The Tragedy of Macbeth

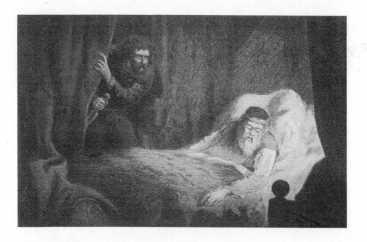

By William Shakespeare

Blackstone Publishing 2019

Table of Contents

Characters in the Play

Three Witches, the Weïrd Sisters
DUNCAN, king of Scotland
MALCOLM, his elder son
DONALBAIN, Duncan's younger son
MACBETH, thane of Glamis
LADY MACBETH
SEYTON, attendant to Macbeth
Three Murderers in Macbeth's service
Attending upon Lady Macbeth
- **A Doctor**
- **A Gentlewoman**

A Porter
BANQUO, commander, with Macbeth, of Duncan's army
FLEANCE, his son
MACDUFF, a Scottish noble
LADY MACDUFF
Their son
Scottish Nobles
- **LENNOX**
- **ROSS**
- **ANGUS**
- **MENTEITH**
- **CAITHNESS**

SIWARD, commander of the English forces
YOUNG SIWARD, Siward's son
A Captain in Duncan's army
An Old Man
A Doctor at the English court
HECATE
Apparitions: **an Armed Head, a Bloody Child, a Crowned Child, and eight nonspeaking kings**
Three Messengers, Three Servants, a Lord, a Soldier
Attendants, a Sewer, Servants, Lords, Thanes, Soldiers (all nonspeaking)

Summary

The play opens with the appearance of trio witches and then later moves towards the military camp where King Duncan gets to hear that his two chief generals Macbeth and Banquo have defeated the Norway army in the war against them. In the tragedy of Lear, the distraught king summons the goddess of Chaos, Hecht. In Macbeth, Hecate appears as an actual character.

Macbeth Meets the three Witches

Three witches decide to confront the great Scottish general Macbeth on his victorious return from a war between Scotland and Norway. They predicted a prophecy to Macbeth that how will he become the Thane of Cawdor and then later the King of Scotland. They also prophesized to Banquo that although he will never become the king he will engender the line of all Scottish King.

Meanwhile, the Scottish king, Duncan, decides that he will confer the title of the Thane of Cawdor on the heroic Macbeth. They were presented with this announcement when they are about to arrive at the camp.

This made Macbeth think about how he might become the king. He decided to invite Duncan to dine and then kill the king. Macbeth's wife agrees to his plan as she was very sure of the witch prophecy.

They planned to make chamberlains of Duncan drink heavily so that they don't remember any of the events and can blame them for the murder of the king. And when the body will be found he will kill the so-called culprits and will then assume to be the Crowned King.

He then murders Duncan assisted by his wife who smears the blood of Duncan on the daggers of the sleeping guards. Macduff discovers the murdered body. As per the plan Macbeth kills the guards insisting that their daggers smeared with Duncan's blood are proof that they committed the murder. Meanwhile, the Sons of Duncan fled away from their country being afraid of their lives.

The crown then passes to Macbeth. He felt insecure with the prophecy which led to the planning in the murder of Banquo and his son Fleance. However, Fleance was not killed and escaped.

He was now incited with paranoia. To overcome his fears, he again visits the witches who said him more prophecy. They said that Macbeth must be aware of his opponent Macduff who also wishes to take the throne. They confronted that Macduff cannot be harmed by any man born of a woman and he is secured until Dunsinane Castle is visited by Birnam Woods.

When he returns home, he comes to know that Macduff has flown away and has joined his hands with Malcom. In fury, Macbeth takes over the castle of Macduff and later orders to kill his wife and children's

Meanwhile, more murders ensue and the bloodied ghost of Banquo appears to him. Lady Macbeth's conscience now begins to torture her and she imagines that she can see her hands covered with blood. She commits suicide and this led Macbeth to go into more despair and depression.

Later Macduff reaches under the security of boughs from the Birnam woods and then defeats Macbeth and becomes king. He also announced that he was not born from his mother rather was "ripped apart from his mother's womb" which made the last two prophecies of the witches true.

Macduff then returned the crown to its rightful heir, Malcom.

The Tragedy of Macbeth

ACT I

SCENE I. A desert place.

Summary: Three witches (a.k.a. the "weird sisters") meet on a foggy heath (an open plain) in Scotland, amidst thunder and lightening. It's all very dramatic and mysterious.

They discuss when they'll meet again, and decide to hook up "When the hurly-burly's done, when the battle's lost and won." In other words, when the fighting that's going on has ended, which apparently will be today, before sunset. Brain snack: Even though the play's speech headings and stage directions refer to these three lovely ladies as "witches," the term "witch" only shows up once in the play.

The sisters are, however, called "weird" six times, but not "weird" like kooky and strange; they're "weird" like "wyrd," an Old English term meaning "fate." Spooky.

They let the audience in on their plan to meet some dude named Macbeth. Title alert! The witches then call out to Graymalkin and Paddock, the witches' "familiars," or spirits (usually animals like cats) that serve the witches.

All three witches then chance, "Fair is foul and foul is fair" before going back about their supernatural business.

Want to see how it all goes down? Check out this video version, from the folks at This is Macbeth.

Thunder and lightning. Enter three Witches

First Witch
When shall we three meet again
In thunder, lightning, or in rain?
Second Witch
When the hurlyburly's done,
When the battle's lost and won.
Third Witch
That will be ere the set of sun.
First Witch
Where the place?
Second Witch
Upon the heath.
Third Witch
There to meet with Macbeth.
First Witch
I come, Graymalkin!
Second Witch
Paddock calls.
Third Witch
Anon.
ALL
Fair is foul, and foul is fair:
Hover through the fog and filthy air.

Exeunt

SCENE II. A camp near Forres.

Summary: Duncan (the King of Scotland), his two sons (Malcolm and Donalbain), and Lennox (a Scottish nobleman) hang out with their attendants at a military camp in Scotland.

King Duncan's forces have been busy fighting against the King of Norway and the traitor, Macdonwald.

A wounded Captain arrives, fresh from the field, where he fought to help Duncan's son, Malcolm, escape capture. What's the news?

Well, says the Captain, the battle was going south fast until brave Macbeth fought through the "swarm" of enemy soldiers and disemboweled the traitorous Macdonwald.

There's some gab about Macbeth's great courage in the face of seemingly impossible adversity and the Captain continues his story: after Macbeth spilled Macdonwald's guts all over the ground, the battle flared up again when the "Norwegian Lord" brought new men to the field, but even this didn't daunt Macbeth and Banquo, who just redoubled their efforts.

Oh, but could someone get the Captain a surgeon? He's kind of bleeding all over the place.

The Thane of Ross arrives from another battle, where Macbeth was also kicking serious butt. Sweno, Norway's king, is not allowed to bury his men until he hands over ten thousand dollars to the Scots.

Duncan then proclaims the traitorous Thane of Cawdor will be executed, and Macbeth, responsible for the victory, shall have his title.

Ross is sent to announce the news to Macbeth.

Alarum within. Enter DUNCAN, MALCOLM, DONALBAIN, LENNOX, with Attendants, meeting a bleeding Sergeant

----

DUNCAN
What bloody man is that? He can report,
As seemeth by his plight, of the revolt
The newest state.
MALCOLM
This is the sergeant
Who like a good and hardy soldier fought
'Gainst my captivity. Hail, brave friend!
Say to the king the knowledge of the broil
As thou didst leave it.

Sergeant
Doubtful it stood;
As two spent swimmers, that do cling together
And choke their art. The merciless Macdonwald--
Worthy to be a rebel, for to that
The multiplying villanies of nature
Do swarm upon him--from the western isles
Of kerns and gallowglasses is supplied;
And fortune, on his damned quarrel smiling,
Show'd like a rebel's whore: but all's too weak:
For brave Macbeth--well he deserves that name--
Disdaining fortune, with his brandish'd steel,
Which smoked with bloody execution,
Like valour's minion carved out his passage
Till he faced the slave;
Which ne'er shook hands, nor bade farewell to him,
Till he unseam'd him from the nave to the chaps,
And fix'd his head upon our battlements.
DUNCAN
O valiant cousin! worthy gentleman!
Sergeant
As whence the sun 'gins his reflection
Shipwrecking storms and direful thunders break,
So from that spring whence comfort seem'd to come
Discomfort swells. Mark, king of Scotland, mark:
No sooner justice had with valour arm'd
Compell'd these skipping kerns to trust their heels,
But the Norweyan lord surveying vantage,
With furbish'd arms and new supplies of men
Began a fresh assault.
DUNCAN
Dismay'd not this
Our captains, Macbeth and Banquo?
Sergeant

Yes;
As sparrows eagles, or the hare the lion.
If I say sooth, I must report they were
As cannons overcharged with double cracks,
so they
Doubly redoubled strokes upon the foe:
Except they meant to bathe in reeking
wounds,
Or memorise another Golgotha,
I cannot tell.
But I am faint, my gashes cry for help.

DUNCAN
So well thy words become thee as thy
wounds;
They smack of honour both. Go get him
surgeons.

Exit Sergeant, attended

Who comes here?

Enter ROSS

MALCOLM
The worthy thane of Ross.

LENNOX
What a haste looks through his eyes! So
should he look
That seems to speak things strange.

ROSS
God save the king!

DUNCAN
Whence camest thou, worthy thane?

ROSS
From Fife, great king;
Where the Norweyan banners flout the sky
And fan our people cold. Norway himself,
With terrible numbers,
Assisted by that most disloyal traitor
The thane of Cawdor, began a dismal
conflict;
Till that Bellona's bridegroom, lapp'd in
proof,
Confronted him with self-comparisons,
Point against point rebellious, arm 'gainst
arm.

Curbing his lavish spirit: and, to conclude,
The victory fell on us.

DUNCAN
Great happiness!

ROSS
That now
Sweno, the Norways' king, craves
composition:
Nor would we deign him burial of his men
Till he disbursed at Saint Colme's inch
Ten thousand dollars to our general use.

DUNCAN
No more that thane of Cawdor shall deceive
Our bosom interest: go pronounce his
present death,
And with his former title greet Macbeth.

ROSS
I'll see it done.

DUNCAN
What he hath lost noble Macbeth hath won.

Exeunt

SCENE III. A heath near Forres.

*Summary: The three witches meet again on
the heath and check in about what
everyone's been up to. Oh, the usual witchy
stuff: one was killing swine; another has
been making some poor sailor's life
miserable.*

*Her sisters are going to help her by
depriving him of sleep and by "drain[ing]
him dry as hay," which means the sailor's
going to have some serious gastro-intestinal
problems and/or that he's going to be unable
to father children.*

*Brain Snack: plenty of people actually
believed in witches the 16th and 17th
centuries, and not the friendly pagan kind,
but the ones who were in the habit of doing
things like whipping up nasty storms and
causing male impotence.*

What, you want more? Shakespeare wrote Macbeth during the reign of King James I of England, who was really interested in witchcraft. He authorized the torture of witches in Scotland in 1591 and also wrote a book on the subject, Daemonologie, in 1603.

Witch #1 also came back with a pilot's thumb, a convenient rhyme for "Macbeth doth come," heralded by "a drum."

Hearing Macbeth's approach, the witches dance around in a circle to "wind up" a "charm."

Macbeth and Banquo show up, and Macbeth delivers his first line: "So foul and fair a day I have not seen." Hmm. Where have we heard that line before?

Banquo notices the witches (they're kind of hard to miss) and speaks to them, using some variety of "You're not from here, are you?"

The witches put their fingers to their lips, but that does not deter the perceptive Banquo from noticing their beards.

Macbeth tells them to speak, and they hail Macbeth as Thane of Glamis, Thane of Cawdor, and future King. Banquo, who apparently took over the narration for these five lines, mentions that Macbeth is "rapt," as if he's in a trance. (Get your highlighter out —this word comes up a lot in the play.)

Banquo asks if the witches will look into his future too. Sure: he'll be lesser and greater than Macbeth, and not too happy, but happier than Macbeth. Oh, and he'll be father to kings, though he will not be a king himself. Great, thanks for clearing that up.

Macbeth says he's already the Thane of Glamis but it's hard to imagine becoming

Thane of Cawdor, especially because the current Thane of Cawdor is alive.

He demands to know where the witches got their information. The witches don't respond, but simply vanish into the foggy, filthy air.

Banquo suggests that maybe they're tripping on some "insane root" but conversation quickly moves on to the big news about their own fates, as promised by the witches. Ross and Angus, two noblemen sent by Duncan (the King), break up the party.

Ross passes on that the King is pleased with Macbeth's battle successes of the day, and announces that the King would like to see him, and also that Macbeth is the new Thane of Cawdor. Macbeth does some private ruminating.

On the one hand, the sisters' first prophecy that Macbeth will be named Thane of Cawdor can't be evil, since it's true. On the other hand, the witch's prophecy could be evil, especially since it's got Macbeth thinking about something naughty. This is where we get the first inkling that Macbeth might be down for a little regicide (fancy word for killing a king).

He says he's just had a really awful and disgusting thought about "murder" that's made him feel a little panicky.

While Macbeth is deep in thought, Banquo comments to Ross and Angus that Macbeth seems "rapt," in a trancelike state.

Macbeth concludes his dramatic musings and says that he's just going to leave things to "chance." If "chance" wants him to be king, then he will be.

They hasten to the King, and Macbeth and Banquo agree to talk more about everything later.

Thunder. Enter the three Witches

First Witch
Where hast thou been, sister?
Second Witch
Killing swine.
Third Witch
Sister, where thou?
First Witch
A sailor's wife had chestnuts in her lap,
And munch'd, and munch'd, and munch'd:--
'Give me,' quoth I:
'Aroint thee, witch!' the rump-fed ronyon cries.
Her husband's to Aleppo gone, master o' the Tiger:
But in a sieve I'll thither sail,
And, like a rat without a tail,
I'll do, I'll do, and I'll do.
Second Witch
I'll give thee a wind.
First Witch
Thou'rt kind.
Third Witch
And I another.
First Witch
I myself have all the other,
And the very ports they blow,
All the quarters that they know
I' the shipman's card.
I will drain him dry as hay:
Sleep shall neither night nor day
Hang upon his pent-house lid;
He shall live a man forbid:
Weary se'nnights nine times nine
Shall he dwindle, peak and pine:
Though his bark cannot be lost,
Yet it shall be tempest-tost.
Look what I have.
Second Witch
Show me, show me.

First Witch
Here I have a pilot's thumb,
Wreck'd as homeward he did come.

Drum within

Third Witch
A drum, a drum!
Macbeth doth come.
ALL
The weird sisters, hand in hand,
Posters of the sea and land,
Thus do go about, about:
Thrice to thine and thrice to mine
And thrice again, to make up nine.
Peace! the charm's wound up.

Enter MACBETH and BANQUO

MACBETH
So foul and fair a day I have not seen.
BANQUO
How far is't call'd to Forres? What are these
So wither'd and so wild in their attire,
That look not like the inhabitants o' the earth,
And yet are on't? Live you? or are you aught
That man may question? You seem to understand me,
By each at once her chappy finger laying
Upon her skinny lips: you should be women,
And yet your beards forbid me to interpret
That you are so.
MACBETH
Speak, if you can: what are you?
First Witch
All hail, Macbeth! hail to thee, thane of Glamis!
Second Witch
All hail, Macbeth, hail to thee, thane of Cawdor!
Third Witch
All hail, Macbeth, thou shalt be king hereafter!
BANQUO

Good sir, why do you start; and seem to fear
Things that do sound so fair? I' the name of truth,
Are ye fantastical, or that indeed
Which outwardly ye show? My noble partner
You greet with present grace and great prediction
Of noble having and of royal hope,
That he seems rapt withal: to me you speak not.
If you can look into the seeds of time,
And say which grain will grow and which will not,
Speak then to me, who neither beg nor fear
Your favours nor your hate.

First Witch
Hail!

Second Witch
Hail!

Third Witch
Hail!

First Witch
Lesser than Macbeth, and greater.

Second Witch
Not so happy, yet much happier.

Third Witch
Thou shalt get kings, though thou be none:
So all hail, Macbeth and Banquo!

First Witch
Banquo and Macbeth, all hail!

MACBETH
Stay, you imperfect speakers, tell me more:
By Sinel's death I know I am thane of Glamis;
But how of Cawdor? the thane of Cawdor lives,
A prosperous gentleman; and to be king
Stands not within the prospect of belief,
No more than to be Cawdor. Say from whence
You owe this strange intelligence? or why
Upon this blasted heath you stop our way
With such prophetic greeting? Speak, I charge you.

Witches vanish

BANQUO
The earth hath bubbles, as the water has,
And these are of them. Whither are they vanish'd?

MACBETH
Into the air; and what seem'd corporal melted
As breath into the wind. Would they had stay'd!

BANQUO
Were such things here as we do speak about?
Or have we eaten on the insane root
That takes the reason prisoner?

MACBETH
Your children shall be kings.

BANQUO
You shall be king.

MACBETH
And thane of Cawdor too: went it not so?

BANQUO
To the selfsame tune and words. Who's here?

Enter ROSS and ANGUS

ROSS
The king hath happily received, Macbeth,
The news of thy success; and when he reads
Thy personal venture in the rebels' fight,
His wonders and his praises do contend
Which should be thine or his: silenced with that,
In viewing o'er the rest o' the selfsame day,
He finds thee in the stout Norweyan ranks,
Nothing afeard of what thyself didst make,
Strange images of death. As thick as hail
Came post with post; and every one did bear
Thy praises in his kingdom's great defence,
And pour'd them down before him.

ANGUS
We are sent
To give thee from our royal master thanks;

Only to herald thee into his sight,
Not pay thee.
ROSS
And, for an earnest of a greater honour,
He bade me, from him, call thee thane of
Cawdor:
In which addition, hail, most worthy thane!
For it is thine.
BANQUO
What, can the devil speak true?
MACBETH
The thane of Cawdor lives: why do you
dress me
In borrow'd robes?
ANGUS
Who was the thane lives yet;
But under heavy judgment bears that life
Which he deserves to lose. Whether he was
combined
With those of Norway, or did line the rebel
With hidden help and vantage, or that with
both
He labour'd in his country's wreck, I know
not;
But treasons capital, confess'd and proved,
Have overthrown him.
MACBETH
[Aside] Glamis, and thane of Cawdor!
The greatest is behind.

To ROSS and ANGUS

Thanks for your pains.

To BANQUO

Do you not hope your children shall be
kings,
When those that gave the thane of Cawdor
to me
Promised no less to them?
BANQUO
That trusted home
Might yet enkindle you unto the crown,
Besides the thane of Cawdor. But 'tis
strange:

And oftentimes, to win us to our harm,
The instruments of darkness tell us truths,
Win us with honest trifles, to betray's
In deepest consequence.
Cousins, a word, I pray you.
MACBETH
[Aside] Two truths are told,
As happy prologues to the swelling act
Of the imperial theme.--I thank you,
gentlemen.

Aside

Cannot be ill, cannot be good: if ill,
Why hath it given me earnest of success,
Commencing in a truth? I am thane of
Cawdor:
If good, why do I yield to that suggestion
Whose horrid image doth unfix my hair
And make my seated heart knock at my ribs,
Against the use of nature? Present fears
Are less than horrible imaginings:
My thought, whose murder yet is but
fantastical,
Shakes so my single state of man that
function
Is smother'd in surmise, and nothing is
But what is not.
BANQUO
Look, how our partner's rapt.
MACBETH
[Aside] If chance will have me king, why,
chance may crown me,
Without my stir.
BANQUO
New horrors come upon him,
Like our strange garments, cleave not to
their mould
But with the aid of use.
MACBETH
[Aside] Come what come may,
Time and the hour runs through the roughest
day.
BANQUO
Worthy Macbeth, we stay upon your leisure.
MACBETH

Give me your favour: my dull brain was wrought
With things forgotten. Kind gentlemen, your pains
Are register'd where every day I turn
The leaf to read them. Let us toward the king.
Think upon what hath chanced, and, at more time,
The interim having weigh'd it, let us speak
Our free hearts each to other.
BANQUO
Very gladly.
MACBETH
Till then, enough. Come, friends.

Exeunt

SCENE IV. Forres. The palace.

Summary: Back to Duncan, who wants to know if the Thane of Cawdor is dead.

He is, and he confessed to being a traitor right before he died.

Whew. Glad that's settled.

Macbeth, Banquo, Ross, and Angus then meet the King. The King is grateful; Macbeth and Banquo pledge their loyalty; group hugs all around.

The King announces that his son Malcolm will be named Prince of Cumberland, which is the last stop before being King of Scotland.

They'll all celebrate the good news at Macbeth's place.

Macbeth trots off, thinking (well, saying, since this is a play) that Malcolm is all that stands in the way of his kingship. He's thinking naughty thoughts again and hopes

nobody can tell that he's got "black and deep desires."

Get the scoop on this scene from its two major players in this interview with Macbeth and Duncan.

Flourish. Enter DUNCAN, MALCOLM, DONALBAIN, LENNOX, and Attendants

DUNCAN
Is execution done on Cawdor? Are not
Those in commission yet return'd?
MALCOLM
My liege,
They are not yet come back. But I have spoke
With one that saw him die: who did report
That very frankly he confess'd his treasons,
Implored your highness' pardon and set forth
A deep repentance: nothing in his life
Became him like the leaving it; he died
As one that had been studied in his death
To throw away the dearest thing he owed,
As 'twere a careless trifle.
DUNCAN
There's no art
To find the mind's construction in the face:
He was a gentleman on whom I built
An absolute trust.

Enter MACBETH, BANQUO, ROSS, and ANGUS

O worthiest cousin!
The sin of my ingratitude even now
Was heavy on me: thou art so far before
That swiftest wing of recompense is slow
To overtake thee. Would thou hadst less deserved,
That the proportion both of thanks and payment
Might have been mine! only I have left to say,
More is thy due than more than all can pay.

MACBETH
The service and the loyalty I owe,
In doing it, pays itself. Your highness' part
Is to receive our duties; and our duties
Are to your throne and state children and
servants,
Which do but what they should, by doing
every thing
Safe toward your love and honour.

DUNCAN
Welcome hither:
I have begun to plant thee, and will labour
To make thee full of growing. Noble
Banquo,
That hast no less deserved, nor must be
known
No less to have done so, let me enfold thee
And hold thee to my heart.

BANQUO
There if I grow,
The harvest is your own.

DUNCAN
My plenteous joys,
Wanton in fulness, seek to hide themselves
In drops of sorrow. Sons, kinsmen, thanes,
And you whose places are the nearest, know
We will establish our estate upon
Our eldest, Malcolm, whom we name
hereafter
The Prince of Cumberland; which honour
must
Not unaccompanied invest him only,
But signs of nobleness, like stars, shall shine
On all deservers. From hence to Inverness,
And bind us further to you.

MACBETH
The rest is labour, which is not used for you:
I'll be myself the harbinger and make joyful
The hearing of my wife with your approach;
So humbly take my leave.

DUNCAN
My worthy Cawdor!

MACBETH
[Aside] The Prince of Cumberland! that is a
step
On which I must fall down, or else o'erleap,

For in my way it lies. Stars, hide your fires;
Let not light see my black and deep desires:
The eye wink at the hand; yet let that be,
Which the eye fears, when it is done, to see.

Exit

DUNCAN
True, worthy Banquo; he is full so valiant,
And in his commendations I am fed;
It is a banquet to me. Let's after him,
Whose care is gone before to bid us
welcome:
It is a peerless kinsman.

Flourish. Exeunt

SCENE V. Inverness. Macbeth's castle.

Summary: *Lady Macbeth receives a letter
from Macbeth, calling her his "dearest
partner of greatness," and telling her of the
witches' prophecy.*

*Lady Macbeth says she's worried her
husband's not up for killing the current king
in order to fulfill the witches' prophecy.
Macbeth, she says, is "too full o'th' milk of
human kindness" and isn't quite wicked
enough to murder Duncan. (Looks like Lady
Macbeth isn't going to leave anything to
"chance.")*

*Lady Macbeth says she's going to browbeat
her husband into action.*

*When a messenger enters and announces
that King Duncan will stay the night at
Inverness as a guest of the Macbeths, Lady
Macbeth tells us it'll be King Duncan's last
night on earth.*

*Then Lady Macbeth delivers one of the most
interesting and astonishing speeches ever.
She calls on spirits to "unsex" her, "make
thick [her] blood," and exchange her breast*

"milk for gall." Translation: Lady Macbeth calls on murderous agents to stop her menstrual flow and change her breast milk for poison (undo all the physical features that make her a reproductive woman). Basically, she suggests that being a woman and a mother could prevent her from committing a violent deed.

When her husband (the guy who's "too full o'th' milk of human kindness") enters the castle, Lady Macbeth tells him that King Duncan's spending the night but he won't be waking up the next morning.

See this scene for yourself, courtesy of the folks at This is Macbeth. And make sure you get Lady Macbeth's take on these events, too.

Enter LADY MACBETH, reading a letter

LADY MACBETH
'They met me in the day of success: and I have
learned by the perfectest report, they have more in
them than mortal knowledge. When I burned in desire
to question them further, they made themselves air,
into which they vanished. Whiles I stood rapt in
the wonder of it, came missives from the king, who
all-hailed me 'Thane of Cawdor;' by which title,
before, these weird sisters saluted me, and referred
me to the coming on of time, with 'Hail, king that
shalt be!' This have I thought good to deliver thee, my dearest partner of greatness, that thou
mightst not lose the dues of rejoicing, by being
ignorant of what greatness is promised thee. Lay it
to thy heart, and farewell.'
Glamis thou art, and Cawdor; and shalt be
What thou art promised: yet do I fear thy nature;
It is too full o' the milk of human kindness
To catch the nearest way: thou wouldst be great;
Art not without ambition, but without
The illness should attend it: what thou wouldst highly,
That wouldst thou holily; wouldst not play false,
And yet wouldst wrongly win: thou'ldst have, great Glamis,
That which cries 'Thus thou must do, if thou have it;
And that which rather thou dost fear to do
Than wishest should be undone.' Hie thee hither,
That I may pour my spirits in thine ear;
And chastise with the valour of my tongue
All that impedes thee from the golden round,
Which fate and metaphysical aid doth seem
To have thee crown'd withal.

Enter a Messenger

What is your tidings?
Messenger
The king comes here to-night.
LADY MACBETH
Thou'rt mad to say it:
Is not thy master with him? who, were't so,
Would have inform'd for preparation.
Messenger
So please you, it is true: our thane is coming:
One of my fellows had the speed of him,
Who, almost dead for breath, had scarcely more
Than would make up his message.
LADY MACBETH

Give him tending;
He brings great news.

Exit Messenger

The raven himself is hoarse
That croaks the fatal entrance of Duncan
Under my battlements. Come, you spirits
That tend on mortal thoughts, unsex me here,
And fill me from the crown to the toe top-full
Of direst cruelty! make thick my blood;
Stop up the access and passage to remorse,
That no compunctious visitings of nature
Shake my fell purpose, nor keep peace between
The effect and it! Come to my woman's breasts,
And take my milk for gall, you murdering ministers,
Wherever in your sightless substances
You wait on nature's mischief! Come, thick night,
And pall thee in the dunnest smoke of hell,
That my keen knife see not the wound it makes,
Nor heaven peep through the blanket of the dark,
To cry 'Hold, hold!'

Enter MACBETH

Great Glamis! worthy Cawdor!
Greater than both, by the all-hail hereafter!
Thy letters have transported me beyond
This ignorant present, and I feel now
The future in the instant.
MACBETH
My dearest love,
Duncan comes here to-night.
LADY MACBETH
And when goes hence?
MACBETH
To-morrow, as he purposes.
LADY MACBETH

O, never
Shall sun that morrow see!
Your face, my thane, is as a book where men
May read strange matters. To beguile the time,
Look like the time; bear welcome in your eye,
Your hand, your tongue: look like the innocent flower,
But be the serpent under't. He that's coming
Must be provided for: and you shall put
This night's great business into my dispatch;
Which shall to all our nights and days to come
Give solely sovereign sway and masterdom.
MACBETH
We will speak further.
LADY MACBETH
Only look up clear;
To alter favour ever is to fear:
Leave all the rest to me.

Exeunt

SCENE VI. Before Macbeth's castle.

Summary: Duncan, his sons, Banquo, and a bevy of noblemen arrive at Glamis Castle (Inverness), complimenting the Lady Macbeth, their "honoured hostess," for her seeming hospitality.

Lady Macbeth is pretty charming here—she says that the Macbeths are grateful for the "honours" bestowed on Macbeth by the king and tells the men to make themselves at home.

There's a whole lot of very formal "You're so gracious." "No you're the one who's so gracious" talk here before Lady Macbeth finally takes the king to see her husband.

Hautboys and torches. Enter DUNCAN, MALCOLM, DONALBAIN, BANQUO, LENNOX, MACDUFF, ROSS, ANGUS, and Attendants

DUNCAN
This castle hath a pleasant seat; the air
Nimbly and sweetly recommends itself
Unto our gentle senses.

BANQUO
This guest of summer,
The temple-haunting martlet, does approve,
By his loved mansionry, that the heaven's breath
Smells wooingly here: no jutty, frieze,
Buttress, nor coign of vantage, but this bird
Hath made his pendent bed and procreant cradle:
Where they most breed and haunt, I have observed,
The air is delicate.

Enter LADY MACBETH

DUNCAN
See, see, our honour'd hostess!
The love that follows us sometime is our trouble,
Which still we thank as love. Herein I teach you
How you shall bid God 'ild us for your pains,
And thank us for your trouble.

LADY MACBETH
All our service
In every point twice done and then done double
Were poor and single business to contend
Against those honours deep and broad wherewith
Your majesty loads our house: for those of old,
And the late dignities heap'd up to them,
We rest your hermits.

DUNCAN
Where's the thane of Cawdor?
We coursed him at the heels, and had a

purpose
To be his purveyor: but he rides well;
And his great love, sharp as his spur, hath holp him
To his home before us. Fair and noble hostess,
We are your guest to-night.

LADY MACBETH
Your servants ever
Have theirs, themselves and what is theirs, in compt,
To make their audit at your highness' pleasure,
Still to return your own.

DUNCAN
Give me your hand;
Conduct me to mine host: we love him highly,
And shall continue our graces towards him.
By your leave, hostess.

Exeunt

SCENE VII. Macbeth's castle.

Summary: Somewhere in the castle Macbeth sits alone, contemplating the murder of King Duncan. And it gets a little complicated. See, if it were simply a matter of killing the king and then moving on without consequences, it wouldn't be a big issue.

The problem is what happens afterward — the whole, being damned to hell thing. It's even worse, because murdering Duncan in Macbeth's own home would be a serious violation of hospitality. He's supposed to protect the king, not murder him. Plus, Duncan is a pretty good king (if not a bit "meek") and heaven is bound to frown upon murdering such a decent fellow.

In then end, Macbeth decides that it's probably not a good idea to commit murder.

*He has no justifiable cause to kill the king
and he admits that he's merely ambitious.*

*And then Lady Macbeth enters.She gives
him a good tongue-lashing, questions his
manhood, and lays out the plan to get
Duncan's guards drunk and frame them for
the murder.*

*If Macbeth can't keep his vow, she says, then
he isn't a man.*

*Macbeth is a little turned on by this show of
strength, and he finally resolves to go
through with the murder.*

----

*Hautboys and torches. Enter a Sewer, and
divers Servants with dishes and service, and
pass over the stage. Then enter MACBETH*

MACBETH
If it were done when 'tis done, then 'twere
well
It were done quickly: if the assassination
Could trammel up the consequence, and
catch
With his surcease success; that but this blow
Might be the be-all and the end-all here,
But here, upon this bank and shoal of time,
We'ld jump the life to come. But in these
cases
We still have judgment here; that we but
teach
Bloody instructions, which, being taught,
return
To plague the inventor: this even-handed
justice
Commends the ingredients of our poison'd
chalice
To our own lips. He's here in double trust;
First, as I am his kinsman and his subject,
Strong both against the deed; then, as his
host,
Who should against his murderer shut the
door,

Not bear the knife myself. Besides, this
Duncan
Hath borne his faculties so meek, hath been
So clear in his great office, that his virtues
Will plead like angels, trumpet-tongued,
against
The deep damnation of his taking-off;
And pity, like a naked new-born babe,
Striding the blast, or heaven's cherubim,
horsed
Upon the sightless couriers of the air,
Shall blow the horrid deed in every eye,
That tears shall drown the wind. I have no
spur
To prick the sides of my intent, but only
Vaulting ambition, which o'erleaps itself
And falls on the other.

Enter LADY MACBETH

How now! what news?
LADY MACBETH
He has almost supp'd: why have you left the
chamber?
MACBETH
Hath he ask'd for me?
LADY MACBETH
Know you not he has?
MACBETH
We will proceed no further in this business:
He hath honour'd me of late; and I have
bought
Golden opinions from all sorts of people,
Which would be worn now in their newest
gloss,
Not cast aside so soon.
LADY MACBETH
Was the hope drunk
Wherein you dress'd yourself? hath it slept
since?
And wakes it now, to look so green and pale
At what it did so freely? From this time
Such I account thy love. Art thou afeard
To be the same in thine own act and valour
As thou art in desire? Wouldst thou have
that

Which thou esteem'st the ornament of life,
And live a coward in thine own esteem,
Letting 'I dare not' wait upon 'I would,'
Like the poor cat i' the adage?

MACBETH
Prithee, peace:
I dare do all that may become a man;
Who dares do more is none.

LADY MACBETH
What beast was't, then,
That made you break this enterprise to me?
When you durst do it, then you were a man;
And, to be more than what you were, you would
Be so much more the man. Nor time nor place
Did then adhere, and yet you would make both:
They have made themselves, and that their fitness now
Does unmake you. I have given suck, and know
How tender 'tis to love the babe that milks me:
I would, while it was smiling in my face,
Have pluck'd my nipple from his boneless gums,
And dash'd the brains out, had I so sworn as you
Have done to this.

MACBETH
If we should fail?

LADY MACBETH
We fail!
But screw your courage to the sticking-place,
And we'll not fail. When Duncan is asleep--
Whereto the rather shall his day's hard journey
Soundly invite him--his two chamberlains
Will I with wine and wassail so convince
That memory, the warder of the brain,
Shall be a fume, and the receipt of reason
A limbeck only: when in swinish sleep
Their drenched natures lie as in a death,
What cannot you and I perform upon
The unguarded Duncan? what not put upon
His spongy officers, who shall bear the guilt
Of our great quell?

MACBETH
Bring forth men-children only;
For thy undaunted mettle should compose
Nothing but males. Will it not be received,
When we have mark'd with blood those sleepy two
Of his own chamber and used their very daggers,
That they have done't?

LADY MACBETH
Who dares receive it other,
As we shall make our griefs and clamour roar
Upon his death?

MACBETH
I am settled, and bend up
Each corporal agent to this terrible feat.
Away, and mock the time with fairest show:
False face must hide what the false heart doth know.

Exeunt

ACT II

SCENE I. Court of Macbeth's castle.

Summary: Banquo and his son, Fleance, are at Macbeth's inner court at Glamis. They're both feeling a little twitchy.

Macbeth then enters with a servant, and Banquo notes that the new Thane of Cawdor (Macbeth) should be resting peacefully considering the good news he got today.

They reminisce about those wacky witches they met the other day, and then everyone leaves Macbeth alone on stage.

Just in time, too, because things are about to get real: Macbeth has a vision of a dagger that points him toward the room where

Duncan sleeps. The dagger turns bloody and Macbeth says the bloody image is a natural result of his bloody thoughts.

A bell rings, which is Lady Macbeth's signal that it's time to rock and roll.

Enter BANQUO, and FLEANCE bearing a torch before him

BANQUO
How goes the night, boy?
FLEANCE
The moon is down; I have not heard the clock.
BANQUO
And she goes down at twelve.
FLEANCE
I take't, 'tis later, sir.
BANQUO
Hold, take my sword. There's husbandry in heaven;
Their candles are all out. Take thee that too.
A heavy summons lies like lead upon me,
And yet I would not sleep: merciful powers,
Restrain in me the cursed thoughts that nature
Gives way to in repose!

Enter MACBETH, and a Servant with a torch

Give me my sword.
Who's there?
MACBETH
A friend.
BANQUO
What, sir, not yet at rest? The king's a-bed:
He hath been in unusual pleasure, and
Sent forth great largess to your offices.
This diamond he greets your wife withal,
By the name of most kind hostess; and shut up
In measureless content.
MACBETH

Being unprepared,
Our will became the servant to defect;
Which else should free have wrought.
BANQUO
All's well.
I dreamt last night of the three weird sisters:
To you they have show'd some truth.
MACBETH
I think not of them:
Yet, when we can entreat an hour to serve,
We would spend it in some words upon that business,
If you would grant the time.
BANQUO
At your kind'st leisure.
MACBETH
If you shall cleave to my consent, when 'tis,
It shall make honour for you.
BANQUO
So I lose none
In seeking to augment it, but still keep
My bosom franchised and allegiance clear,
I shall be counsell'd.
MACBETH
Good repose the while!
BANQUO
Thanks, sir: the like to you!

Exeunt BANQUO and FLEANCE

MACBETH
Go bid thy mistress, when my drink is ready,
She strike upon the bell. Get thee to bed.

Exit Servant

Is this a dagger which I see before me,
The handle toward my hand? Come, let me clutch thee.
I have thee not, and yet I see thee still.
Art thou not, fatal vision, sensible
To feeling as to sight? or art thou but
A dagger of the mind, a false creation,
Proceeding from the heat-oppressed brain?
I see thee yet, in form as palpable
As this which now I draw.

Thou marshall'st me the way that I was
going;
And such an instrument I was to use.
Mine eyes are made the fools o' the other
senses,
Or else worth all the rest; I see thee still,
And on thy blade and dudgeon gouts of
blood,
Which was not so before. There's no such
thing:
It is the bloody business which informs
Thus to mine eyes. Now o'er the one
halfworld
Nature seems dead, and wicked dreams
abuse
The curtain'd sleep; witchcraft celebrates
Pale Hecate's offerings, and wither'd murder,
Alarum'd by his sentinel, the wolf,
Whose howl's his watch, thus with his
stealthy pace.
With Tarquin's ravishing strides, towards his
design
Moves like a ghost. Thou sure and firm-set
earth,
Hear not my steps, which way they walk, for
fear
Thy very stones prate of my whereabout,
And take the present horror from the time,
Which now suits with it. Whiles I threat, he
lives:
Words to the heat of deeds too cold breath
gives.

A bell rings

I go, and it is done; the bell invites me.
Hear it not, Duncan; for it is a knell
That summons thee to heaven or to hell.

Exit

SCENE II. The same.

Summary: *Lady Macbeth is alone on stage.
She tells us that she drugged the King's
guards and would've even killed Duncan*

*herself, if he hadn't looked so much like her
father in his sleep. Apparently, she's all
family values now.*

*Macbeth enters with bloody hands and a
weird story: two separate people staying in
the castle woke up while he was in the act.
One cried, "Murder!" but they both went
back to sleep after saying their prayers.*

*Macbeth is disturbed that he couldn't say
"Amen" when they said, "God bless us." He
could have used the blessing, given how he
recently damned his soul by killing the King.
Lady Macbeth is of the "If you don't think
about, it will go away" school of thought,
but Macbeth is still clearly disturbed at
having killed a sleeping old man for his own
selfish gain.*

*There's also a little problem where he heard
voices saying things like "Macbeth does
murder sleep!"*

*Lady Macbeth tries to get her husband to
focus on the matter at hand, which is
framing the King's attendants.*

*He won't do it himself, so she takes the
daggers from him, smears the attendants
with Duncan's blood, and plants the
weapons. Come on. That would never fool
CSI: Cawdor.*

*As Macbeth philosophizes about his guilty
hands, Lady Macbeth comes back, having
done her part.*

*She hears a knock at the door, and hurries
Macbeth to bed so that (1) they don't look
suspicious, and (2) they can do a little
washing up before all the "Oh no! The king
is dead" morning hullabaloo.*

*Macbeth regrets killing Duncan —he says
he wishes that all the knocking at the door*

would "wake Duncan" from his eternal sleep.Sorry, dude. No take-backsies with murder.

Enter LADY MACBETH

LADY MACBETH
That which hath made them drunk hath made me bold;
What hath quench'd them hath given me fire.
Hark! Peace!
It was the owl that shriek'd, the fatal bellman,
Which gives the stern'st good-night. He is about it:
The doors are open; and the surfeited grooms
Do mock their charge with snores: I have drugg'd
their possets,
That death and nature do contend about them,
Whether they live or die.

MACBETH
[Within] Who's there? what, ho!

LADY MACBETH
Alack, I am afraid they have awaked,
And 'tis not done. The attempt and not the deed
Confounds us. Hark! I laid their daggers ready;
He could not miss 'em. Had he not resembled
My father as he slept, I had done't.

Enter MACBETH

My husband!

MACBETH
I have done the deed. Didst thou not hear a noise?

LADY MACBETH
I heard the owl scream and the crickets cry.
Did not you speak?

MACBETH
When?

LADY MACBETH
Now.

MACBETH
As I descended?

LADY MACBETH
Ay.

MACBETH
Hark!
Who lies i' the second chamber?

LADY MACBETH
Donalbain.

MACBETH
This is a sorry sight.

Looking on his hands

LADY MACBETH
A foolish thought, to say a sorry sight.

MACBETH
There's one did laugh in's sleep, and one cried
'Murder!'
That they did wake each other: I stood and heard them:
But they did say their prayers, and address'd them
Again to sleep.

LADY MACBETH
There are two lodged together.

MACBETH
One cried 'God bless us!' and 'Amen' the other;
As they had seen me with these hangman's hands.
Listening their fear, I could not say 'Amen,'
When they did say 'God bless us!'

LADY MACBETH
Consider it not so deeply.

MACBETH
But wherefore could not I pronounce 'Amen'?
I had most need of blessing, and 'Amen'
Stuck in my throat.

LADY MACBETH

These deeds must not be thought
After these ways; so, it will make us mad.

MACBETH
Methought I heard a voice cry 'Sleep no more!
Macbeth does murder sleep', the innocent sleep,
Sleep that knits up the ravell'd sleeve of care,
The death of each day's life, sore labour's bath,
Balm of hurt minds, great nature's second course,
Chief nourisher in life's feast,--

LADY MACBETH
What do you mean?

MACBETH
Still it cried 'Sleep no more!' to all the house:
'Glamis hath murder'd sleep, and therefore Cawdor
Shall sleep no more; Macbeth shall sleep no more.'

LADY MACBETH
Who was it that thus cried? Why, worthy thane,
You do unbend your noble strength, to think
So brainsickly of things. Go get some water,
And wash this filthy witness from your hand.
Why did you bring these daggers from the place?
They must lie there: go carry them; and smear
The sleepy grooms with blood.

MACBETH
I'll go no more:
I am afraid to think what I have done;
Look on't again I dare not.

LADY MACBETH
Infirm of purpose!
Give me the daggers: the sleeping and the dead
Are but as pictures: 'tis the eye of childhood
That fears a painted devil. If he do bleed,
I'll gild the faces of the grooms withal;
For it must seem their guilt.

Exit. Knocking within

MACBETH
Whence is that knocking?
How is't with me, when every noise appals me?
What hands are here? ha! they pluck out mine eyes.
Will all great Neptune's ocean wash this blood
Clean from my hand? No, this my hand will rather
The multitudinous seas in incarnadine,
Making the green one red.

Re-enter LADY MACBETH

LADY MACBETH
My hands are of your colour; but I shame
To wear a heart so white.

Knocking within

I hear a knocking
At the south entry: retire we to our chamber;
A little water clears us of this deed:
How easy is it, then! Your constancy
Hath left you unattended.

Knocking within

Hark! more knocking.
Get on your nightgown, lest occasion call us,
And show us to be watchers. Be not lost
So poorly in your thoughts.

MACBETH
To know my deed, 'twere best not know myself.

Knocking within

Wake Duncan with thy knocking! I would thou couldst!

Exeunt

SCENE III. The same.

Summary: *Now that Shakespeare's given us a murder and a lot of spooky crazy talk from Macbeth, we're obviously ready for a brief, comedic interlude.*

There's a ton of knocking and the Porter (the guy who's supposed to answer the door) does a lot of joking around about what it would be like to be a porter of "hellgate."

Apparently, a porter in hell would be a busy guy since there are so many evil and corrupt people in the world. The Porter runs through a bunch of scenarios for who could be at the door (a farmer, a con-man, a tailor) and he has witty remarks for all of them. Things like: "I hope you brought a handkerchief— you're going to get sweaty!" and "You can heat up your iron in here!" (Ba-DUM-bum.)

It's Macduff and Lennox, who have come to fetch the king.

The laugh-a-minute Porter makes a bunch of jokes about how drinking an excessive amount of alcohol, like he's been doing, makes a man frisky —but it also detracts from his "performance" in the sack, not to mention turning his nose red and making him have to pee.

Enter Macbeth, the picture of sleepy innocence while he makes small talk with Lennox and sends Macduff to wake Duncan.

Lennox notes that some spooky things have been happening all night —he heard a bunch of screams, there was a little earthquake, and the fire in his chimney blew out.

Yep, says Macbeth, it was a pretty rough night. But not as rough as it was for Duncan, who Macduff has just found murdered.

Macduff tells Macbeth and Lennox to go see Duncan's body for themselves. It's too gruesome for him to describe, except to say that viewing the scene is like looking at a Gorgon. (Medusa was a Gorgon, and when men looked at her they turned to stone, Chamber of Secrets style.) Macduff sounds the alarm to wake the whole castle, both by yelling his head off and calling for a bell to be rung.

Everyone starts running around, Lady Macbeth and Banquo show up, and then Macbeth starts a way-too-eager eulogy about the King's great virtues.

So, who murdered the king? Lennox thinks that the drunken guards covered in the King's blood and holding their daggers are a good bet.

Macbeth casually announces that he killed both of the guards in a fit of pious rage, out of his love for the King.

Apparently, no one thinks it's weird that the guards went to sleep with the bloody daggers in hand.

Lady Macbeth, upon hearing that Macbeth has done this, wisely stages a diversion—or maybe she really does nearly faint in response to her husband's stupidity. In either case, she needs to be escorted out. (Taking credit for the killing of the guards was not part of her plan).

Donalbain and Malcolm privately decide that they probably shouldn't stay in the house where their dad was killed. Good thinking. A+ for self-preservation. The rest of the men say they suspect treason and agree to meet in the hall to discuss the situation, pronto.

Malcolm will go to England and Donalbain to Ireland, making it more difficult to murder them both.

The dead king's sons slip out, unnoticed, while everyone else gets dressed and prepares to talk this thing through.

Knocking within. Enter a Porter

Porter
Here's a knocking indeed! If a
man were porter of hell-gate, he should have
old turning the key.

Knocking within

Knock,
knock, knock! Who's there, i' the name of
Beelzebub? Here's a farmer, that hanged
himself on the expectation of plenty: come in
time; have napkins enow about you; here
you'll sweat for't.

Knocking within

Knock,
knock! Who's there, in the other devil's
name? Faith, here's an equivocator, that could
swear in both the scales against either scale;
who committed treason enough for God's sake,
yet could not equivocate to heaven: O, come
in, equivocator.

Knocking within

Knock,
knock, knock! Who's there? Faith, here's an
English tailor come hither, for stealing out of
a French hose: come in, tailor; here you may
roast your goose.

Knocking within

Knock,
knock; never at quiet! What are you? But
this place is too cold for hell. I'll devil-porter
it no further: I had thought to have let in
some of all professions that go the primrose
way to the everlasting bonfire.

Knocking within

Anon, anon! I pray you, remember the
porter.

Opens the gate

Enter MACDUFF and LENNOX

MACDUFF
Was it so late, friend, ere you went to bed,
That you do lie so late?
Porter
'Faith sir, we were carousing till the
second cock: and drink, sir, is a great
provoker of three things.
MACDUFF
What three things does drink especially
provoke?
Porter
Marry, sir, nose-painting, sleep, and
urine. Lechery, sir, it provokes, and
unprovokes;
it provokes the desire, but it takes
away the performance: therefore, much drink
may be said to be an equivocator with
lechery:

it makes him, and it mars him; it sets
him on, and it takes him off; it persuades
him,
and disheartens him; makes him stand to,
and
not stand to; in conclusion, equivocates him
in a sleep, and, giving him the lie, leaves
him.

MACDUFF
I believe drink gave thee the lie last night.

Porter
That it did, sir, i' the very throat on
me: but I requited him for his lie; and, I
think, being too strong for him, though he
took
up my legs sometime, yet I made a shift to
cast
him.

MACDUFF
Is thy master stirring?

Enter MACBETH

Our knocking has awaked him; here he
comes.

LENNOX
Good morrow, noble sir.

MACBETH
Good morrow, both.

MACDUFF
Is the king stirring, worthy thane?

MACBETH
Not yet.

MACDUFF
He did command me to call timely on him:
I have almost slipp'd the hour.

MACBETH
I'll bring you to him.

MACDUFF
I know this is a joyful trouble to you;
But yet 'tis one.

MACBETH
The labour we delight in physics pain.
This is the door.

MACDUFF

I'll make so bold to call,
For 'tis my limited service.

Exit

LENNOX
Goes the king hence to-day?

MACBETH
He does: he did appoint so.

LENNOX
The night has been unruly: where we lay,
Our chimneys were blown down; and, as
they say,
Lamentings heard i' the air; strange screams
of death,
And prophesying with accents terrible
Of dire combustion and confused events
New hatch'd to the woeful time: the obscure
bird
Clamour'd the livelong night: some say, the
earth
Was feverous and did shake.

MACBETH
'Twas a rough night.

LENNOX
My young remembrance cannot parallel
A fellow to it.

Re-enter MACDUFF

MACDUFF
O horror, horror, horror! Tongue nor heart
Cannot conceive nor name thee!

MACBETH LENNOX
What's the matter.

MACDUFF
Confusion now hath made his masterpiece!
Most sacrilegious murder hath broke ope
The Lord's anointed temple, and stole thence
The life o' the building!

MACBETH
What is 't you say? the life?

LENNOX
Mean you his majesty?

MACDUFF

Approach the chamber, and destroy your sight
With a new Gorgon: do not bid me speak;
See, and then speak yourselves.

Exeunt MACBETH and LENNOX

Awake, awake!
Ring the alarum-bell. Murder and treason!
Banquo and Donalbain! Malcolm! awake!
Shake off this downy sleep, death's counterfeit,
And look on death itself! up, up, and see
The great doom's image! Malcolm! Banquo!
As from your graves rise up, and walk like sprites,
To countenance this horror! Ring the bell.

Bell rings

Enter LADY MACBETH

LADY MACBETH
What's the business,
That such a hideous trumpet calls to parley
The sleepers of the house? speak, speak!
MACDUFF
O gentle lady,
'Tis not for you to hear what I can speak:
The repetition, in a woman's ear,
Would murder as it fell.

Enter BANQUO

O Banquo, Banquo,
Our royal master 's murder'd!
LADY MACBETH
Woe, alas!
What, in our house?
BANQUO
Too cruel any where.
Dear Duff, I prithee, contradict thyself,
And say it is not so.

Re-enter MACBETH and LENNOX, with ROSS

MACBETH
Had I but died an hour before this chance,
I had lived a blessed time; for, from this instant,
There 's nothing serious in mortality:
All is but toys: renown and grace is dead;
The wine of life is drawn, and the mere lees
Is left this vault to brag of.

Enter MALCOLM and DONALBAIN

DONALBAIN
What is amiss?
MACBETH
You are, and do not know't:
The spring, the head, the fountain of your blood
Is stopp'd; the very source of it is stopp'd.
MACDUFF
Your royal father 's murder'd.
MALCOLM
O, by whom?
LENNOX
Those of his chamber, as it seem'd, had done 't:
Their hands and faces were an badged with blood;
So were their daggers, which unwiped we found
Upon their pillows:
They stared, and were distracted; no man's life
Was to be trusted with them.
MACBETH
O, yet I do repent me of my fury,
That I did kill them.
MACDUFF
Wherefore did you so?
MACBETH
Who can be wise, amazed, temperate and furious,
Loyal and neutral, in a moment? No man:
The expedition my violent love
Outrun the pauser, reason. Here lay Duncan,
His silver skin laced with his golden blood;
And his gash'd stabs look'd like a breach in

nature
For ruin's wasteful entrance: there, the murderers,
Steep'd in the colours of their trade, their daggers
Unmannerly breech'd with gore: who could refrain,
That had a heart to love, and in that heart
Courage to make 's love kno wn?

LADY MACBETH
Help me hence, ho!

MACDUFF
Look to the lady.

MALCOLM
[Aside to DONALBAIN] Why do we hold our tongues,
That most may claim this argument for ours?

DONALBAIN
[Aside to MALCOLM] What should be spoken here,
where our fate,
Hid in an auger-hole, may rush, and seize us?
Let 's away;
Our tears are not yet brew'd.

MALCOLM
[Aside to DONALBAIN] Nor our strong sorrow
Upon the foot of motion.

BANQUO
Look to the lady:

LADY MACBETH is carried out

And when we have our naked frailties hid,
That suffer in exposure, let us meet,
And question this most bloody piece of work,
To know it further. Fears and scruples shake us:
In the great hand of God I stand; and thence
Against the undivulged pretence I fight
Of treasonous malice.

MACDUFF
And so do I.

ALL
So all.

MACBETH
Let's briefly put on manly readiness,
And meet i' the hall together.

ALL
Well contented.

Exeunt all but Malcolm and Donalbain.

MALCOLM
What will you do? Let's not consort with them:
To show an unfelt sorrow is an office
Which the false man does easy. I'll to England.

DONALBAIN
To Ireland, I; our separated fortune
Shall keep us both the safer: where we are,
There's daggers in men's smiles: the near in blood,
The nearer bloody.

MALCOLM
This murderous shaft that's shot
Hath not yet lighted, and our safest way
Is to avoid the aim. Therefore, to horse;
And let us not be dainty of leave-taking,
But shift away: there's warrant in that theft
Which steals itself, when there's no mercy left.

Exeunt

SCENE IV. Outside Macbeth's castle.

Summary: Ross chats with a conveniently placed wise old man, who is disturbed by the night's strange events—both the King's murder and the weird things going on in nature.

Ross says the heavens are clearly troubled by the unnatural regicide: even though it's the middle of the day, it's completely dark outside; an owl murdered a hawk; Duncan's horses ate each other. Okay, that seriously sounds like something out of The Exorcist.

Macduff, yet another Scottish nobleman, offers some exposition, too: he says the dead guards "were bribed" to murder the king (wrong); that Malcolm and Donalbain look pretty suspicious, having left town so quickly and all (can't argue with that, even though we know better); that Macbeth is on his way to Scone to be crowned King; and that Duncan is being put in a freshly dug grave.

Time for a new act.

Enter ROSS and an old Man

Old Man
Threescore and ten I can remember well:
Within the volume of which time I have seen
Hours dreadful and things strange; but this sore night
Hath trifled former knowings.
ROSS
Ah, good father,
Thou seest, the heavens, as troubled with man's act,
Threaten his bloody stage: by the clock, 'tis day,
And yet dark night strangles the travelling lamp:
Is't night's predominance, or the day's shame,
That darkness does the face of earth entomb,
When living light should kiss it?
Old Man
'Tis unnatural,
Even like the deed that's done. On Tuesday last,
A falcon, towering in her pride of place,
Was by a mousing owl hawk'd at and kill'd.
ROSS
And Duncan's horses--a thing most strange and certain--

Beauteous and swift, the minions of their race,
Turn'd wild in nature, broke their stalls, flung out,
Contending 'gainst obedience, as they would make
War with mankind.
Old Man
'Tis said they eat each other.
ROSS
They did so, to the amazement of mine eyes
That look'd upon't. Here comes the good Macduff.

Enter MACDUFF

How goes the world, sir, now?
MACDUFF
Why, see you not?
ROSS
Is't known who did this more than bloody deed?
MACDUFF
Those that Macbeth hath slain.
ROSS
Alas, the day!
What good could they pretend?
MACDUFF
They were suborn'd:
Malcolm and Donalbain, the king's two sons,
Are stol'n away and fled; which puts upon them
Suspicion of the deed.
ROSS
'Gainst nature still!
Thriftless ambition, that wilt ravin up
Thine own life's means! Then 'tis most like
The sovereignty will fall upon Macbeth.
MACDUFF
He is already named, and gone to Scone
To be invested.
ROSS
Where is Duncan's body?
MACDUFF

Carried to Colmekill,
The sacred storehouse of his predecessors,
And guardian of their bones.
ROSS
Will you to Scone?
MACDUFF
No, cousin, I'll to Fife.
ROSS
Well, I will thither.
MACDUFF
Well, may you see things well done there:
adieu!
Lest our old robes sit easier than our new!
ROSS
Farewell, father.
Old Man
God's benison go with you; and with those
That would make good of bad, and friends
of foes!

Exeunt

ACT III

SCENE I. Forres. The palace.

*Summary: At Macbeth's new palace in
Forres, Banquo, alone on stage, delivers a
soliloquy: he's totally suspicious of
Macbeth. But he does take the time to note
that his part of the prophecy, regarding his
royal seed, will also probably come true.*

*Banquo pipes down when the newly crowned
Macbeth, his lovely Queen, and a posse of
noblemen enter the room.*

*Macbeth sweet talks Banquo, calling him his
honored guest and requesting his presence
at a fancy banquet to be held that night.
Banquo says he will, of course, do whatever
Macbeth asks. However, he won't be around
to offer any advice this afternoon as he has
errands to run.*

*Macbeth oh-so-casually asks what Banquo
will be up to, and finds out that he'll be
riding off somewhere before the dinner, but
that he'll definitely be back in time for the
feast.*

*Having obtained the information he needs,
Macbeth changes the subject to the fact that
the "bloody" Malcolm and Donalbain are
suspiciously missing, and respectively
hiding out with new friends in Ireland and
England. Plus, it seems that Duncan's sons
are busy "not confessing" to Duncan's
murder —instead, they're spreading nasty
rumors about their father's death.*

*Macbeth adds a little BTW as Banquo
leaves, asking if his son, Fleance, will be
riding along with him that evening. Fleance
will indeed be going, and upon hearing this,
Macbeth bids them farewell.*

*Everyone except for Macbeth and a servant
leave the room.*

*Macbeth has the servant call in the men he
has waiting at the gate.*

*Left to himself, Macbeth launches into a
long speech about why it's necessary and
good to kill his friend, Banquo. Uh, okay.*

*Macbeth is worried about Banquo's noble
nature, wisdom, and valor. Plus, if the rest
of the witches' prophecy comes true,
Macbeth figures that he'll have sold his soul
to the devil (by killing Duncan) only for
Banquo's kids to take his crown.*

*He concludes his speech by inviting fate to
wrestle with him, and says he won't give up
until he's won or dead. Hm. It seems like it's
getting a whole lot easier for Macbeth to
think about murder, don't you think?*

The two men at the gate are brought in, and we discover that Macbeth intends for them to murder Banquo and his son while on their ride.

Macbeth speechifies to the two murderers about how Banquo is their enemy and anything bad that has ever happened to them is surely Banquo's fault. Macbeth says that no turn-the-other-cheek Christianity is necessary here.

The murderers respond by saying that they are only "men," and then Macbeth uses the technique he learned while being berated by his own wife: he claims they're not real men if they're not brave enough to murder a man for their own good.

Um...okay, say the henchmen. We'll do it. Their lives are pretty bad anyway. They're fine with taking a chance on eternal damnation.

Macbeth says that Banquo is his enemy, too, and he'd do the kingly thing and just have him publicly killed, except that they have a lot of mutual friends, which might make things a little awkward at parties.

The murderers again say they'll do it, and Macbeth says he'll tell them where they need to be and when. Oh, and they'll have to kill the Fleance, too. Macbeth will be in touch shortly, but right now he has to go get ready for a dinner party. After they leave, Macbeth delivers a nice rhyming couplet indicating that if Banquo's soul is headed to heaven, it will arrive there tonight.

Enter BANQUO
BANQUO

Thou hast it now: king, Cawdor, Glamis, all,
As the weird women promised, and, I fear,
Thou play'dst most foully for't: yet it was said
It should not stand in thy posterity,
But that myself should be the root and father
Of many kings. If there come truth from them--
As upon thee, Macbeth, their speeches shine--
Why, by the verities on thee made good,
May they not be my oracles as well,
And set me up in hope? But hush! no more.

Sennet sounded. Enter MACBETH, as king, LADY MACBETH, as queen, LENNOX, ROSS, Lords, Ladies, and Attendants

MACBETH
Here's our chief guest.
LADY MACBETH
If he had been forgotten,
It had been as a gap in our great feast,
And all-thing unbecoming.
MACBETH
To-night we hold a solemn supper sir,
And I'll request your presence.
BANQUO
Let your highness
Command upon me; to the which my duties
Are with a most indissoluble tie
For ever knit.
MACBETH
Ride you this afternoon?
BANQUO
Ay, my good lord.
MACBETH
We should have else desired your good advice,
Which still hath been both grave and prosperous,
In this day's council; but we'll take to-morrow.
Is't far you ride?
BANQUO

As far, my lord, as will fill up the time
'Twixt this and supper: go not my horse the
better,
I must become a borrower of the night
For a dark hour or twain.
MACBETH
Fail not our feast.
BANQUO
My lord, I will not.
MACBETH
We hear, our bloody cousins are bestow'd
In England and in Ireland, not confessing
Their cruel parricide, filling their hearers
With strange invention: but of that to-
morrow,
When therewithal we shall have cause of
state
Craving us jointly. Hie you to horse: adieu,
Till you return at night. Goes Fleance with
you?
BANQUO
Ay, my good lord: our time does call upon
's.
MACBETH
I wish your horses swift and sure of foot;
And so I do commend you to their backs.
Farewell.

Exit BANQUO

Let every man be master of his time
Till seven at night: to make society
The sweeter welcome, we will keep ourself
Till supper-time alone: while then, God be
with you!

Exeunt all but MACBETH, and an attendant

Sirrah, a word with you: attend those men
Our pleasure?
ATTENDANT
They are, my lord, without the palace gate.
MACBETH
Bring them before us.

Exit Attendant

To be thus is nothing;
But to be safely thus.--Our fears in Banquo
Stick deep; and in his royalty of nature
Reigns that which would be fear'd: 'tis much
he dares;
And, to that dauntless temper of his mind,
He hath a wisdom that doth guide his valour
To act in safety. There is none but he
Whose being I do fear: and, under him,
My Genius is rebuked; as, it is said,
Mark Antony's was by Caesar. He chid the
sisters
When first they put the name of king upon
me,
And bade them speak to him: then prophet-
like
They hail'd him father to a line of kings:
Upon my head they placed a fruitless crown,
And put a barren sceptre in my gripe,
Thence to be wrench'd with an unlineal
hand,
No son of mine succeeding. If 't be so,
For Banquo's issue have I filed my mind;
For them the gracious Duncan have I
murder'd;
Put rancours in the vessel of my peace
Only for them; and mine eternal jewel
Given to the common enemy of man,
To make them kings, the seed of Banquo
kings!
Rather than so, come fate into the list.
And champion me to the utterance! Who's
there!

Re-enter Attendant, with two Murderers

Now go to the door, and stay there till we
call.

Exit Attendant

Was it not yesterday we spoke together?
First Murderer
It was, so please your highness.
MACBETH

Well then, now
Have you consider'd of my speeches? Know
That it was he in the times past which held
you
So under fortune, which you thought had
been
Our innocent self: this I made good to you
In our last conference, pass'd in probation
with you,
How you were borne in hand, how cross'd,
the instruments,
Who wrought with them, and all things else
that might
To half a soul and to a notion crazed
Say 'Thus did Banquo.'

First Murderer
You made it known to us.

MACBETH
I did so, and went further, which is now
Our point of second meeting. Do you find
Your patience so predominant in your nature
That you can let this go? Are you so
gospell'd
To pray for this good man and for his issue,
Whose heavy hand hath bow'd you to the
grave
And beggar'd yours for ever?

First Murderer
We are men, my liege.

MACBETH
Ay, in the catalogue ye go for men;
As hounds and greyhounds, mongrels,
spaniels, curs,
Shoughs, water-rugs and demi-wolves, are
clept
All by the name of dogs: the valued file
Distinguishes the swift, the slow, the subtle,
The housekeeper, the hunter, every one
According to the gift which bounteous
nature
Hath in him closed; whereby he does receive
Particular addition. from the bill
That writes them all alike: and so of men.
Now, if you have a station in the file,
Not i' the worst rank of manhood, say 't;
And I will put that business in your bosoms,

Whose execution takes your enemy off,
Grapples you to the heart and love of us,
Who wear our health but sickly in his life,
Which in his death were perfect.

Second Murderer
I am one, my liege,
Whom the vile blows and buffets of the
world
Have so incensed that I am reckless what
I do to spite the world.

First Murderer
And I another
So weary with disasters, tugg'd with fortune,
That I would set my lie on any chance,
To mend it, or be rid on't.

MACBETH
Both of you
Know Banquo was your enemy.

Both Murderers
True, my lord.

MACBETH
So is he mine; and in such bloody distance,
That every minute of his being thrusts
Against my near'st of life: and though I
could
With barefaced power sweep him from my
sight
And bid my will avouch it, yet I must not,
For certain friends that are both his and
mine,
Whose loves I may not drop, but wail his
fall
Who I myself struck down; and thence it is,
That I to your assistance do make love,
Masking the business from the common eye
For sundry weighty reasons.

Second Murderer
We shall, my lord,
Perform what you command us.

First Murderer
Though our lives--

MACBETH
Your spirits shine through you. Within this
hour at most
I will advise you where to plant yourselves;
Acquaint you with the perfect spy o' the

time,
The moment on't; for't must be done to-
night,
And something from the palace; always
thought
That I require a clearness: and with him--
To leave no rubs nor botches in the work--
Fleance his son, that keeps him company,
Whose absence is no less material to me
Than is his father's, must embrace the fate
Of that dark hour. Resolve yourselves apart:
I'll come to you anon.
Both Murderers
We are resolved, my lord.
MACBETH
I'll call upon you straight: abide within.

Exeunt Murderers

It is concluded. Banquo, thy soul's flight,
If it find heaven, must find it out to-night.

Exit

SCENE II. The palace.

Summary: *Lady Macbeth asks a servant if Banquo is already gone. When she realizes he has, she asks the servant to get Macbeth for a little chat.*

Macbeth comes along, and Lady Macbeth tells him to look more chipper and not dwell on dark thoughts, as "what's done is done."

Macbeth points out they've merely scorched the snake, not killed it. Macbeth compares dead Duncan's death as a state preferable to his; at least Duncan doesn't have to worry about loose ends.

All right, Debbie Downer, says Lady Macbeth; just chill out there.

Macbeth says he will. And he tells his wife she should say a lot of really nice things

about Banquo, flatter him, and maybe even flirt with him a little. That will help hide their guilt.

Lady Macbeth tells him he has to stop talking about what they've done.

But Macbeth says that as long as Banquo and Fleance are alive, he's going to be paranoid. He can't stop these dark thoughts and his fear of being found out, and his worries about Banquo's son getting his crown.

Lady Macbeth says they won't live forever, which leads Macbeth to say, "Hmm. That's true. In fact..."

In fact, what? Lady Macbeth wants to know what her husband is plotting.

Macbeth dodges her question, saying it's better for her to "be innocent" and not know his plans until they're accomplished and she can applaud him for it. Gee. It seems like Lady Macbeth no longer gets any say in her husband's affairs.

Macbeth appeals to nature to let night's black agents do their thing, and then he exits with Lady Macbeth.

Enter LADY MACBETH and a Servant

LADY MACBETH
Is Banquo gone from court?
Servant
Ay, madam, but returns again to-night.
LADY MACBETH
Say to the king, I would attend his leisure
For a few words.
Servant
Madam, I will.

Exit

LADY MACBETH
Nought's had, all's spent,
Where our desire is got without content:
'Tis safer to be that which we destroy
Than by destruction dwell in doubtful joy.

Enter MACBETH

How now, my lord! why do you keep alone,
Of sorriest fancies your companions making,
Using those thoughts which should indeed
have died
With them they think on? Things without all
remedy
Should be without regard: what's done is
done.
MACBETH
We have scotch'd the snake, not kill'd it:
She'll close and be herself, whilst our poor
malice
Remains in danger of her former tooth.
But let the frame of things disjoint, both the
worlds suffer,
Ere we will eat our meal in fear and sleep
In the affliction of these terrible dreams
That shake us nightly: better be with the
dead,
Whom we, to gain our peace, have sent to
peace,
Than on the torture of the mind to lie
In restless ecstasy. Duncan is in his grave;
After life's fitful fever he sleeps well;
Treason has done his worst: nor steel, nor
poison,
Malice domestic, foreign levy, nothing,
Can touch him further.
LADY MACBETH
Come on;
Gentle my lord, sleek o'er your rugged
looks;
Be bright and jovial among your guests to-
night.
MACBETH
So shall I, love; and so, I pray, be you:
Let your remembrance apply to Banquo;
Present him eminence, both with eye and
tongue:
Unsafe the while, that we
Must lave our honours in these flattering
streams,
And make our faces vizards to our hearts,
Disguising what they are.
LADY MACBETH
You must leave this.
MACBETH
O, full of scorpions is my mind, dear wife!
Thou know'st that Banquo, and his Fleance,
lives.
LADY MACBETH
But in them nature's copy's not eterne.
MACBETH
There's comfort yet; they are assailable;
Then be thou jocund: ere the bat hath flown
His cloister'd flight, ere to black Hecate's
summons
The shard-borne beetle with his drowsy
hums
Hath rung night's yawning peal, there shall
be done
A deed of dreadful note.
LADY MACBETH
What's to be done?
MACBETH
Be innocent of the knowledge, dearest
chuck,
Till thou applaud the deed. Come, seeling
night,
Scarf up the tender eye of pitiful day;
And with thy bloody and invisible hand
Cancel and tear to pieces that great bond
Which keeps me pale! Light thickens; and
the crow
Makes wing to the rooky wood:
Good things of day begin to droop and
drowse;
While night's black agents to their preys do
rouse.
Thou marvell'st at my words: but hold thee
still;
Things bad begun make strong themselves
by ill.
So, prithee, go with me.

Exeunt

SCENE III. A park near the palace.

Summary: *At a park near the palace, the two murderers are joined by a third, which is a little fishy. He says Macbeth sent him, but the First and Second Murderers didn't seem to be expecting anyone else. Check out this fun blog post for some theories about who the Third Murderer may (and may not) be.*

Banquo and Fleance approach on horseback and dismount to walk the mile to the palace, as usual. Conveniently, they have a torch—good for seeing by.

Banquo starts up with a friendly "it looks like rain" conversation and is promptly stabbed.

While being stabbed, he denounces the treachery and encourages Fleance to run away and eventually take revenge.

In the meantime, the torch has gone out, and Fleance takes advantage of the darkness to escape.

With Banquo dead and Fleance on the run, the murderers head off to the dinner party to report the half of the job they've done.

Enter three Murderers

First Murderer
But who did bid thee join with us?
Third Murderer
Macbeth.
Second Murderer
He needs not our mistrust, since he delivers
Our offices and what we have to do
To the direction just.
First Murderer

Then stand with us.
The west yet glimmers with some streaks of day:
Now spurs the lated traveller apace
To gain the timely inn; and near approaches
The subject of our watch.
Third Murderer
Hark! I hear horses.
BANQUO
[Within] Give us a light there, ho!
Second Murderer
Then 'tis he: the rest
That are within the note of expectation
Already are i' the court.
First Murderer
His horses go about.
Third Murderer
Almost a mile: but he does usually,
So all men do, from hence to the palace gate
Make it their walk.
Second Murderer
A light, a light!

Enter BANQUO, and FLEANCE with a torch

Third Murderer
'Tis he.
First Murderer
Stand to't.
BANQUO
It will be rain to-night.
First Murderer
Let it come down.

They set upon BANQUO

BANQUO
O, treachery! Fly, good Fleance, fly, fly, fly!
Thou mayst revenge. O slave!

Dies. FLEANCE escapes

Third Murderer
Who did strike out the light?
First Murderer

Wast not the way?
Third Murderer
There's but one down; the son is fled.
Second Murderer
We have lost
Best half of our affair.
First Murderer
Well, let's away, and say how much is done.

Exeunt

SCENE IV. The same. Hall in the palace.

Summary: Meanwhile, back at the dinner party, the Macbeths make a big show of welcoming their guests.

The first murderer enters as everyone is being seated. Macbeth darts off to see the first murderer, who informs him that they've slit Banquo's throat, but that Fleance has escaped.

Ooh. Not good. Macbeth is pretty sure that this is really going to tick Fleance off.

And now the fun begins: Banquo's ghost shows up. Because the ghost is silent, he gets to creep around quite a bit before anyone notices.

While everyone is busy not noticing, Macbeth raises a toast and calls special attention to Banquo's absence. He hopes Banquo is just running late or being rude and that nothing horrible has happened to him. What a thoughtful guy.

This is particularly hilarious given the presence...Banquo's ghost.

Again Macbeth is invited to sit, and in the spot they've reserved for him sits...Banquo's ghost. Naturally, Macbeth goes into a fit, and the lords all take notice. Lady Macbeth, always a quick thinker, excuses her husband

for these "momentary" fits he has had since childhood.

She urges them to keep eating, and then corners Macbeth, who is still hysterical.

Lady Macbeth asks if Macbeth is a man, because he's not acting like one so much as he is acting like a sissy. She tells him to get it together—there's nothing but a stool in front of him. This "ghost" business is all in his head.

Meanwhile, Macbeth is discoursing with the ghost that only he sees, and then it disappears. He swears to Lady Macbeth that the ghost was there, and then laments that it used to be that when you dashed a man's brains out he would die. Now, apparently, instead of dying people come back and steal your seat at the table. Sheesh. The nerve!

Everything is just getting back to normal when the ghost reappears. Again Macbeth calls out a toast to the missing Banquo (he's just asking for it now). When he sees that the ghost has returned, Macbeth screams at him for being so spooky. He says if Banquo were to appear in any physical form—even a Russian bear—Macbeth would take him on, no problem. The ghost leaves again and Macbeth tells everyone to stay put.

Lady Macbeth lets him know that he's killed the mood. It's pretty clear the party's over.

Macbeth tries to recover, and he even questions everyone else asking how they can be so calm in the face of such horrible sights. Um...what sights? they want to know.

Lady Macbeth tells the concerned lords to leave immediately. Pronto. NOW.

After they exit, Macbeth philosophizes that

*blood will have blood. In other words, this
ain't over yet.*

*Morning is now approaching, and Macbeth
points out that Macduff never showed at the
party. He lets out that he has had a spy in
Macduff's house. He promises to go to the
witches the next day, and says that he's so
far into this bloody business that there's no
turning back now.*

*Lady Macbeth suggests that maybe he just
needs a good night's sleep, and so they go
off to bed. Sweet dreams, you crazy kids!*

----

*A banquet prepared. Enter MACBETH,
LADY MACBETH, ROSS, LENNOX, Lords,
and Attendants*

MACBETH
You know your own degrees; sit down: at
first
And last the hearty welcome.
Lords
Thanks to your majesty.
MACBETH
Ourself will mingle with society,
And play the humble host.
Our hostess keeps her state, but in best time
We will require her welcome.
LADY MACBETH
Pronounce it for me, sir, to all our friends;
For my heart speaks they are welcome.

First Murderer appears at the door

MACBETH
See, they encounter thee with their hearts'
thanks.
Both sides are even: here I'll sit i' the midst:
Be large in mirth; anon we'll drink a
measure
The table round.

Approaching the door

There's blood on thy face.
First Murderer
'Tis Banquo's then.
MACBETH
'Tis better thee without than he within.
Is he dispatch'd?
First Murderer
My lord, his throat is cut; that I did for him.
MACBETH
Thou art the best o' the cut-throats: yet he's
good
That did the like for Fleance: if thou didst it,
Thou art the nonpareil.
First Murderer
Most royal sir,
Fleance is 'scaped.
MACBETH
Then comes my fit again: I had else been
perfect,
Whole as the marble, founded as the rock,
As broad and general as the casing air:
But now I am cabin'd, cribb'd, confined,
bound in
To saucy doubts and fears. But Banquo's
safe?
First Murderer
Ay, my good lord: safe in a ditch he bides,
With twenty trenched gashes on his head;
The least a death to nature.
MACBETH
Thanks for that:
There the grown serpent lies; the worm
that's fled
Hath nature that in time will venom breed,
No teeth for the present. Get thee gone: to-
morrow
We'll hear, ourselves, again.

Exit Murderer

LADY MACBETH
My royal lord,
You do not give the cheer: the feast is sold
That is not often vouch'd, while 'tis a-
making,
'Tis given with welcome: to feed were best

at home;
From thence the sauce to meat is ceremony;
Meeting were bare without it.
MACBETH
Sweet remembrancer!
Now, good digestion wait on appetite,
And health on both!
LENNOX
May't please your highness sit.

*The GHOST OF BANQUO enters, and sits
in MACBETH's place*

MACBETH
Here had we now our country's honour
roof'd,
Were the graced person of our Banquo
present;
Who may I rather challenge for unkindness
Than pity for mischance!
ROSS
His absence, sir,
Lays blame upon his promise. Please't your
highness
To grace us with your royal company.
MACBETH
The table's full.
LENNOX
Here is a place reserved, sir.
MACBETH
Where?
LENNOX
Here, my good lord. What is't that moves
your highness?
MACBETH
Which of you have done this?
Lords
What, my good lord?
MACBETH
Thou canst not say I did it: never shake
Thy gory locks at me.
ROSS
Gentlemen, rise: his highness is not well.
LADY MACBETH
Sit, worthy friends: my lord is often thus,
And hath been from his youth: pray you,

keep seat;
The fit is momentary; upon a thought
He will again be well: if much you note him,
You shall offend him and extend his
passion:
Feed, and regard him not. Are you a man?
MACBETH
Ay, and a bold one, that dare look on that
Which might appal the devil.
LADY MACBETH
O proper stuff!
This is the very painting of your fear:
This is the air-drawn dagger which, you
said,
Led you to Duncan. O, these flaws and
starts,
Impostors to true fear, would well become
A woman's story at a winter's fire,
Authorized by her grandam. Shame itself!
Why do you make such faces? When all's
done,
You look but on a stool.
MACBETH
Prithee, see there! behold! look! lo!
how say you?
Why, what care I? If thou canst nod, speak
too.
If charnel-houses and our graves must send
Those that we bury back, our monuments
Shall be the maws of kites.

GHOST OF BANQUO vanishes

LADY MACBETH
What, quite unmann'd in folly?
MACBETH
If I stand here, I saw him.
LADY MACBETH
Fie, for shame!
MACBETH
Blood hath been shed ere now, i' the olden
time,
Ere human statute purged the gentle weal;
Ay, and since too, murders have been
perform'd
Too terrible for the ear: the times have been,

That, when the brains were out, the man would die,
And there an end; but now they rise again,
With twenty mortal murders on their crowns,
And push us from our stools: this is more strange
Than such a murder is.

LADY MACBETH
My worthy lord,
Your noble friends do lack you.

MACBETH
I do forget.
Do not muse at me, my most worthy friends,
I have a strange infirmity, which is nothing
To those that know me. Come, love and health to all;
Then I'll sit down. Give me some wine; fill full.
I drink to the general joy o' the whole table,
And to our dear friend Banquo, whom we miss;
Would he were here! to all, and him, we thirst,
And all to all.

Lords
Our duties, and the pledge.

Re-enter GHOST OF BANQUO

MACBETH
Avaunt! and quit my sight! let the earth hide thee!
Thy bones are marrowless, thy blood is cold;
Thou hast no speculation in those eyes
Which thou dost glare with!

LADY MACBETH
Think of this, good peers,
But as a thing of custom: 'tis no other;
Only it spoils the pleasure of the time.

MACBETH
What man dare, I dare:
Approach thou like the rugged Russian bear,
The arm'd rhinoceros, or the Hyrcan tiger;
Take any shape but that, and my firm nerves
Shall never tremble: or be alive again,
And dare me to the desert with thy sword;
If trembling I inhabit then, protest me
The baby of a girl. Hence, horrible shadow!
Unreal mockery, hence!

GHOST OF BANQUO vanishes

Why, so: being gone,
I am a man again. Pray you, sit still.

LADY MACBETH
You have displaced the mirth, broke the good meeting,
With most admired disorder.

MACBETH
Can such things be,
And overcome us like a summer's cloud,
Without our special wonder? You make me strange
Even to the disposition that I owe,
When now I think you can behold such sights,
And keep the natural ruby of your cheeks,
When mine is blanched with fear.

ROSS
What sights, my lord?

LADY MACBETH
I pray you, speak not; he grows worse and worse;
Question enrages him. At once, good night:
Stand not upon the order of your going,
But go at once.

LENNOX
Good night; and better health
Attend his majesty!

LADY MACBETH
A kind good night to all!

Exeunt all but MACBETH and LADY MACBETH

MACBETH
It will have blood; they say, blood will have blood:
Stones have been known to move and trees to speak;
Augurs and understood relations have

By magot-pies and choughs and rooks
brought forth
The secret'st man of blood. What is the
night?
LADY MACBETH
Almost at odds with morning, which is
which.
MACBETH
How say'st thou, that Macduff denies his
person
At our great bidding?
LADY MACBETH
Did you send to him, sir?
MACBETH
I hear it by the way; but I will send:
There's not a one of them but in his house
I keep a servant fee'd. I will to-morrow,
And betimes I will, to the weird sisters:
More shall they speak; for now I am bent to
know,
By the worst means, the worst. For mine
own good,
All causes shall give way: I am in blood
Stepp'd in so far that, should I wade no
more,
Returning were as tedious as go o'er:
Strange things I have in head, that will to
hand;
Which must be acted ere they may be
scann'd.
LADY MACBETH
You lack the season of all natures, sleep.
MACBETH
Come, we'll to sleep. My strange and self-
abuse
Is the initiate fear that wants hard use:
We are yet but young in deed.

Exeunt

SCENE V. A Heath.

*Summary: The witches again meet at an
open place, this time with Hecate, the
goddess of witches, who looks pretty angry.*

*Hecate lays into the weird sisters in a
lengthy, rhyming speech that sounds a bit
like a nursery rhyme.*

*She's super irritated that they were meddling
in the affairs of Macbeth without consulting
her first, as she could've done a better job.
Also, she points out, Macbeth isn't devoted
to them, only to himself.*

*But, fine, Hecate will clean up this mess. She
tells them to all meet in the morning, when
Macbeth will come to know his destiny,
whatever that means.*

*Then there's a catchy witch song and dance,
and everyone exits after Hecate.*

*FYI: Some literary critics believe that these
scene is way too hokey to be Shakespeare's
work, so it must have been added to the play
some time between the time the play was
first written (1606) and its publication in the
first folio (1623), which was after
Shakespeare's death (1616). A fellow
playwright, Thomas Middleton, may have
written the snazzy songs in this scene.*

----

*Thunder. Enter the three Witches meeting
HECATE*

First Witch
Why, how now, Hecate! you look angerly.
HECATE
Have I not reason, beldams as you are,
Saucy and overbold? How did you dare
To trade and traffic with Macbeth
In riddles and affairs of death;
And I, the mistress of your charms,
The close contriver of all harms,
Was never call'd to bear my part,

Or show the glory of our art?
And, which is worse, all you have done
Hath been but for a wayward son,
Spiteful and wrathful, who, as others do,
Loves for his own ends, not for you.
But make amends now: get you gone,
And at the pit of Acheron
Meet me i' the morning: thither he
Will come to know his destiny:
Your vessels and your spells provide,
Your charms and every thing beside.
I am for the air; this night I'll spend
Unto a dismal and a fatal end:
Great business must be wrought ere noon:
Upon the corner of the moon
There hangs a vaporous drop profound;
I'll catch it ere it come to ground:
And that distill'd by magic sleights
Shall raise such artificial sprites
As by the strength of their illusion
Shall draw him on to his confusion:
He shall spurn fate, scorn death, and bear
He hopes 'bove wisdom, grace and fear:
And you all know, security
Is mortals' chiefest enemy.

Music and a song within: 'Come away, come away,' & c

Hark! I am call'd; my little spirit, see,
Sits in a foggy cloud, and stays for me.

Exit

First Witch
Come, let's make haste; she'll soon be back
again.

Exeunt

SCENE VI. Forres. The palace.

Summary: Meanwhile, elsewhere in Scotland:

The nobleman Lennox discusses Scotland's plight with another lord. Isn't it weird that Duncan was murdered, that his run-away sons were blamed, that Banquo has now been murdered, that his run-away son (Fleance) is being blamed, and that everyone has a major case of déjà vu? Plus, the murders of Banquo and Duncan were too conveniently grieved by Macbeth, who had the most to gain from the deaths.

Lennox refers to Macbeth as a "tyrant," and then asks the other Lord if he knows where Macduff has gone off to.

Turns out Macduff has joined Malcolm in England.

Malcolm and Macduff are doing a pretty good job of convincing the oh-so gracious and "pious" King Edward of England, along with some English noblemen, to help them in the fight against Macbeth, the tyrant.

FYI: Shakespeare's giving England and King Edward the Confessor (1042-1066) some serious props here.

The two noblemen pray that Malcolm and Macduff might be successful and restore some order to the kingdom, even though news of the planned rebellion has reached Macbeth and he's preparing for war.

Sorry to say, it's not looking too good for Macbeth at this point.

Enter LENNOX and another Lord

LENNOX
My former speeches have but hit your thoughts,
Which can interpret further: only, I say,
Things have been strangely borne. The gracious Duncan

Was pitied of Macbeth: marry, he was dead:
And the right-valiant Banquo walk'd too late;
Whom, you may say, if't please you, Fleance kill'd,
For Fleance fled: men must not walk too late.
Who cannot want the thought how monstrous
It was for Malcolm and for Donalbain
To kill their gracious father? damned fact!
How it did grieve Macbeth! did he not straight
In pious rage the two delinquents tear,
That were the slaves of drink and thralls of sleep?
Was not that nobly done? Ay, and wisely too;
For 'twould have anger'd any heart alive
To hear the men deny't. So that, I say,
He has borne all things well: and I do think
That had he Duncan's sons under his key--
As, an't please heaven, he shall not--they should find
What 'twere to kill a father; so should Fleance.
But, peace! for from broad words and 'cause he fail'd
His presence at the tyrant's feast, I hear
Macduff lives in disgrace: sir, can you tell
Where he bestows himself?

Lord
The son of Duncan,
From whom this tyrant holds the due of birth
Lives in the English court, and is received
Of the most pious Edward with such grace
That the malevolence of fortune nothing
Takes from his high respect: thither Macduff
Is gone to pray the holy king, upon his aid
To wake Northumberland and warlike Siward:
That, by the help of these--with Him above
To ratify the work--we may again
Give to our tables meat, sleep to our nights,
Free from our feasts and banquets bloody knives,

Do faithful homage and receive free honours:
All which we pine for now: and this report
Hath so exasperate the king that he
Prepares for some attempt of war.

LENNOX
Sent he to Macduff?

Lord
He did: and with an absolute 'Sir, not I,'
The cloudy messenger turns me his back,
And hums, as who should say 'You'll rue the time
That clogs me with this answer.'

LENNOX
And that well might
Advise him to a caution, to hold what distance
His wisdom can provide. Some holy angel
Fly to the court of England and unfold
His message ere he come, that a swift blessing
May soon return to this our suffering country
Under a hand accursed!

Lord
I'll send my prayers with him.

Exeunt

ACT IV

SCENE I. A cavern. In the middle, a boiling cauldron.

Summary: On a dark and stormy night, the three witches are hanging out in a cave roasting marshmallows and chanting spells around a boiling cauldron, into which they cast all sorts of nasty bits, from lizard's leg to the finger of stillborn baby.

Hecate enters, pleased with the witches' more serious approach this time around. After Hecate exits, the Second With announces "something wicked this way comes."

Not surprisingly, Macbeth promptly follows. (So does a Ray Bradbury novel and cinematic adaptation, but not for another few centuries.)

Macbeth gives the witches some props for being able to control the weather and conjure crazy winds that batter churches, cause huge ocean waves to "swallow" ships, destroy crops, topple castles, and so on. (Hmm...this reminds us of Act I, scene iii, where the witches say they're going to punish a sailor's wife by whipping up a nasty little storm for her husband, who is at sea.)

Macbeth says he has some more questions about his future and he wants some answers from the weird sisters, pronto.

The witches add some more ingredients to the cauldron, and then apparitions begin to appear, each addressing Macbeth.

First, an armed head warns him to beware of Macduff.

The second apparition is a bloody child who says that Macbeth won't be harmed by anyone who was "of woman born." Um, well...that's pretty much everyone, right? Including Macduff. So really Macbeth figures he has nothing to fear. He welcomes this good but figures he might as well have Macduff killed anyway—you know, just to be sure.

The third apparition is a child wearing a crown and holding a tree in his hand. The child promises that Macbeth won't be conquered until Birnam Wood marches to Dunsinane. This seems about as unlikely as Macduff not being born of a woman.

Given all of this, Macbeth feels safe that he won't be conquered in the upcoming war.

But again, to be on the safe side, he still asks if Banquo's children will ever rule the kingdom.

He is warned to ask no more questions.

He demands to be answered anyway.

Macbeth is not pleased when he's shown a line of eight kings, the last of which holds a mirror that reflects on many more such kings. One of the kings in the mirror happens to be holding two orbs.

Time for a History Snack: King James I of England (a.k.a. King James VI of Scotland) traced his lineage back to Banquo and, at his coronation ceremony in England (1603) James held two orbs (one representing England and one representing Scotland). Quite a coincidence, don't you think?

The apparitions disappear and the witches tease Macbeth for looking horrible when he saw his future destruction. The witches do yet another song and dance routine and they vanish.

Enter Lennox to find a perplexed Macbeth. Lennox tells Macbeth the news that Macduff has definitely run away to England, presumably to get some help for a rebellion.

Get your highlighter out because this next bit is important: Macbeth says that from now on, he's going to act immediately on whatever thought enters his mind: "From this moment / The very firstlings of my heart shall be / The firstlings of my hand." In other words, no more thinking and contemplating about the pros and cons of being bad – he's just going to do whatever the heck he feels like doing.

Starting with... wiping out Macduff's entire family, especially his kids, since Macbeth

*doesn't ever want to see any little Macduffs
running around.*

Thunder. Enter the three Witches
First Witch
Thrice the brinded cat hath mew'd.
Second Witch
Thrice and once the hedge-pig whined.
Third Witch
Harpier cries 'Tis time, 'tis time.
First Witch
Round about the cauldron go;
In the poison'd entrails throw.
Toad, that under cold stone
Days and nights has thirty-one
Swelter'd venom sleeping got,
Boil thou first i' the charmed pot.
ALL
Double, double toil and trouble;
Fire burn, and cauldron bubble.
Second Witch
Fillet of a fenny snake,
In the cauldron boil and bake;
Eye of newt and toe of frog,
Wool of bat and tongue of dog,
Adder's fork and blind-worm's sting,
Lizard's leg and owlet's wing,
For a charm of powerful trouble,
Like a hell-broth boil and bubble.
ALL
Double, double toil and trouble;
Fire burn and cauldron bubble.
Third Witch
Scale of dragon, tooth of wolf,
Witches' mummy, maw and gulf
Of the ravin'd salt-sea shark,
Root of hemlock digg'd i' the dark,
Liver of blaspheming Jew,
Gall of goat, and slips of yew
Silver'd in the moon's eclipse,
Nose of Turk and Tartar's lips,
Finger of birth-strangled babe
Ditch-deliver'd by a drab,
Make the gruel thick and slab:

Add thereto a tiger's chaudron,
For the ingredients of our cauldron.
ALL
Double, double toil and trouble;
Fire burn and cauldron bubble.
Second Witch
Cool it with a baboon's blood,
Then the charm is firm and good.

Enter HECATE to the other three Witches

HECATE
O well done! I commend your pains;
And every one shall share i' the gains;
And now about the cauldron sing,
Live elves and fairies in a ring,
Enchanting all that you put in.

Music and a song: 'Black spirits,' & c

HECATE retires

Second Witch
By the pricking of my thumbs,
Something wicked this way comes.
Open, locks,
Whoever knocks!

Enter MACBETH

MACBETH
How now, you secret, black, and midnight
hags!
What is't you do?
ALL
A deed without a name.
MACBETH
I conjure you, by that which you profess,
Howe'er you come to know it, answer me:
Though you untie the winds and let them
fight
Against the churches; though the yesty
waves
Confound and swallow navigation up;
Though bladed corn be lodged and trees
blown down;

Though castles topple on their warders'
heads;
Though palaces and pyramids do slope
Their heads to their foundations; though the
treasure
Of nature's germens tumble all together,
Even till destruction sicken; answer me
To what I ask you.
First Witch
Speak.
Second Witch
Demand.
Third Witch
We'll answer.
First Witch
Say, if thou'dst rather hear it from our
mouths,
Or from our masters?
MACBETH
Call 'em; let me see 'em.
First Witch
Pour in sow's blood, that hath eaten
Her nine farrow; grease that's sweaten
From the murderer's gibbet throw
Into the flame.
ALL
Come, high or low;
Thyself and office deftly show!

Thunder. First Apparition: an armed Head

MACBETH
Tell me, thou unknown power,--
First Witch
He knows thy thought:
Hear his speech, but say thou nought.
First Apparition
Macbeth! Macbeth! Macbeth! beware
Macduff;
Beware the thane of Fife. Dismiss me.
Enough.

Descends

MACBETH

Whate'er thou art, for thy good caution,
thanks;
Thou hast harp'd my fear aright: but one
word more,--
First Witch
He will not be commanded: here's another,
More potent than the first.

Thunder. Second Apparition: A bloody Child

Second Apparition
Macbeth! Macbeth! Macbeth!
MACBETH
Had I three ears, I'ld hear thee.
Second Apparition
Be bloody, bold, and resolute; laugh to scorn
The power of man, for none of woman born
Shall harm Macbeth.

Descends

MACBETH
Then live, Macduff: what need I fear of
thee?
But yet I'll make assurance double sure,
And take a bond of fate: thou shalt not live;
That I may tell pale-hearted fear it lies,
And sleep in spite of thunder.

*Thunder. Third Apparition: a Child
crowned, with a tree in his hand*

What is this
That rises like the issue of a king,
And wears upon his baby-brow the round
And top of sovereignty?
ALL
Listen, but speak not to't.
Third Apparition
Be lion-mettled, proud; and take no care
Who chafes, who frets, or where conspirers
are:
Macbeth shall never vanquish'd be until
Great Birnam wood to high Dunsinane hill
Shall come against him.

Descends

MACBETH
That will never be
Who can impress the forest, bid the tree
Unfix his earth-bound root? Sweet
bodements! good!
Rebellion's head, rise never till the wood
Of Birnam rise, and our high-placed
Macbeth
Shall live the lease of nature, pay his breath
To time and mortal custom. Yet my heart
Throbs to know one thing: tell me, if your
art
Can tell so much: shall Banquo's issue ever
Reign in this kingdom?
ALL
Seek to know no more.
MACBETH
I will be satisfied: deny me this,
And an eternal curse fall on you! Let me
know.
Why sinks that cauldron? and what noise is
this?

Hautboys

First Witch
Show!
Second Witch
Show!
Third Witch
Show!
ALL
Show his eyes, and grieve his heart;
Come like shadows, so depart!

*A show of Eight Kings, the last with a glass
in his hand; GHOST OF BANQUO
following*

MACBETH
Thou art too like the spirit of Banquo: down!
Thy crown does sear mine eye-balls. And
thy hair,
Thou other gold-bound brow, is like the
first.
A third is like the former. Filthy hags!
Why do you show me this? A fourth! Start,
eyes!
What, will the line stretch out to the crack of
doom?
Another yet! A seventh! I'll see no more:
And yet the eighth appears, who bears a
glass
Which shows me many more; and some I
see
That two-fold balls and treble scepters carry:
Horrible sight! Now, I see, 'tis true;
For the blood-bolter'd Banquo smiles upon
me,
And points at them for his.

Apparitions vanish

What, is this so?
First Witch
Ay, sir, all this is so: but why
Stands Macbeth thus amazedly?
Come, sisters, cheer we up his sprites,
And show the best of our delights:
I'll charm the air to give a sound,
While you perform your antic round:
That this great king may kindly say,
Our duties did his welcome pay.

*Music. The witches dance and then vanish,
with HECATE*

MACBETH
Where are they? Gone? Let this pernicious
hour
Stand aye accursed in the calendar!
Come in, without there!

Enter LENNOX

LENNOX
What's your grace's will?
MACBETH
Saw you the weird sisters?
LENNOX

No, my lord.
MACBETH
Came they not by you?
LENNOX
No, indeed, my lord.
MACBETH
Infected be the air whereon they ride;
And damn'd all those that trust them! I did hear
The galloping of horse: who was't came by?
LENNOX
'Tis two or three, my lord, that bring you word
Macduff is fled to England.
MACBETH
Fled to England!
LENNOX
Ay, my good lord.
MACBETH
Time, thou anticipatest my dread exploits:
The flighty purpose never is o'ertook
Unless the deed go with it; from this moment
The very firstlings of my heart shall be
The firstlings of my hand. And even now,
To crown my thoughts with acts, be it thought and done:
The castle of Macduff I will surprise;
Seize upon Fife; give to the edge o' the sword
His wife, his babes, and all unfortunate souls
That trace him in his line. No boasting like a fool;
This deed I'll do before this purpose cool.
But no more sights!--Where are these gentlemen?
Come, bring me where they are.

Exeunt

SCENE II. Fife. Macduff's castle.

Summary: *At Fife, in Macduff's castle, Lady Macduff is lamenting to Ross that her husband has run away, which, sure makes him look suspicious.*

Also, abandoning your family with no defense is seriously uncool. It's cool, Ross says. Macduff had his reasons.

Lady Macduff then has a funny bit of banter with her young son about how his father is dead. He doesn't believe her, and they go on to discuss whether or not she should buy a new husband at the market as well as what happens to traitors. The kid is pretty witty. He suggests that there are enough bad men in the world to beat up the good men and hang them, so really, the traitors shouldn't be too concerned about their fates. Then he adds that he knows his dad isn't dead. If he were, Lady Macduff would be crying.

Lady Macduff is entertained by her son's cheekiness, but the conversation comes to an abrupt end when a messenger enters advising her to flee with her children.

Since she's innocent, she sees no reason to leave. Then again, she thinks, this is Earth, where sometimes people are praised for doing evil things and punished for doing good things. So being innocent may not be a good reason to stay put.

Unfortunately, in the time it takes her to figure this out, the murderers have arrived.

One of the murderers says they're looking for Macduff, who is a traitor.

Macduff's son retorts, is stabbed, and then dies, leaving the murderers to pursue mom.

Enter LADY MACDUFF, her Son, and ROSS

LADY MACDUFF
What had he done, to make him fly the land?
ROSS
You must have patience, madam.

LADY MACDUFF
He had none:
His flight was madness: when our actions do not,
Our fears do make us traitors.
ROSS
You know not
Whether it was his wisdom or his fear.
LADY MACDUFF
Wisdom! to leave his wife, to leave his babes,
His mansion and his titles in a place
From whence himself does fly? He loves us not;
He wants the natural touch: for the poor wren,
The most diminutive of birds, will fight,
Her young ones in her nest, against the owl.
All is the fear and nothing is the love;
As little is the wisdom, where the flight
So runs against all reason.
ROSS
My dearest coz,
I pray you, school yourself: but for your husband,
He is noble, wise, judicious, and best knows
The fits o' the season. I dare not speak much further;
But cruel are the times, when we are traitors
And do not know ourselves, when we hold rumour
From what we fear, yet know not what we fear,
But float upon a wild and violent sea
Each way and move. I take my leave of you:
Shall not be long but I'll be here again:
Things at the worst will cease, or else climb upward
To what they were before. My pretty cousin,
Blessing upon you!
LADY MACDUFF
Father'd he is, and yet he's fatherless.
ROSS
I am so much a fool, should I stay longer,
It would be my disgrace and your

discomfort:
I take my leave at once.

Exit

LADY MACDUFF
Sirrah, your father's dead;
And what will you do now? How will you live?
Son
As birds do, mother.
LADY MACDUFF
What, with worms and flies?
Son
With what I get, I mean; and so do they.
LADY MACDUFF
Poor bird! thou'ldst never fear the net nor lime,
The pitfall nor the gin.
Son
Why should I, mother? Poor birds they are not set for.
My father is not dead, for all your saying.
LADY MACDUFF
Yes, he is dead; how wilt thou do for a father?
Son
Nay, how will you do for a husband?
LADY MACDUFF
Why, I can buy me twenty at any market.
Son
Then you'll buy 'em to sell again.
LADY MACDUFF
Thou speak'st with all thy wit: and yet, i' faith,
With wit enough for thee.
Son
Was my father a traitor, mother?
LADY MACDUFF
Ay, that he was.
Son
What is a traitor?
LADY MACDUFF
Why, one that swears and lies.
Son
And be all traitors that do so?

LADY MACDUFF
Every one that does so is a traitor, and must
be hanged.
Son
And must they all be hanged that swear and
lie?
LADY MACDUFF
Every one.
Son
Who must hang them?
LADY MACDUFF
Why, the honest men.
Son
Then the liars and swearers are fools,
for there are liars and swearers enow to beat
the honest men and hang up them.
LADY MACDUFF
Now, God help thee, poor monkey!
But how wilt thou do for a father?
Son
If he were dead, you'ld weep for
him: if you would not, it were a good sign
that I should quickly have a new father.
LADY MACDUFF
Poor prattler, how thou talk'st!

Enter a Messenger

Messenger
Bless you, fair dame! I am not to you
known,
Though in your state of honour I am perfect.
I doubt some danger does approach you
nearly:
If you will take a homely man's advice,
Be not found here; hence, with your little
ones.
To fright you thus, methinks, I am too
savage;
To do worse to you were fell cruelty,
Which is too nigh your person. Heaven
preserve you!
I dare abide no longer.

Exit

LADY MACDUFF
Whither should I fly?
I have done no harm. But I remember now
I am in this earthly world; where to do harm
Is often laudable, to do good sometime
Accounted dangerous folly: why then, alas,
Do I put up that womanly defence,
To say I have done no harm?

Enter Murderers

What are these faces?
First Murderer
Where is your husband?
LADY MACDUFF
I hope, in no place so unsanctified
Where such as thou mayst find him.
First Murderer
He's a traitor.
Son
Thou liest, thou shag-hair'd villain!
First Murderer
What, you egg!

Stabbing him

Young fry of treachery!
Son
He has kill'd me, mother:
Run away, I pray you!

Dies

Exit LADY MACDUFF, crying 'Murder!'
Exeunt Murderers, following her

**SCENE III. England. Before the King's
palace.**

*Summary: Near King Edward's palace in
England, Malcolm and Macduff brainstorm
about Scotland's plight under the tyrannous
Macbeth.*

*Malcolm suggests finding a nice shady spot
where they can cry their eyes out. Macduff's*

got a better idea: maybe they should whip out their swords and fight like "men" against the good-for-nothing Macbeth.

Sure, that's an okay idea, says Malcolm; but he's worried Macduff might have something to gain by turning on him, (Malcolm) and betraying him to Macbeth. Besides, Macduff doesn't seem like a loyal guy these days, having abandoned his family back in Scotland and all. No man, Macduff says; I'm totally loyal.

Still, Malcolm's a little paranoid so he decides to test Macduff by suggesting that even he, Malcolm, might make a poor king, were they to defeat Macbeth. Scotland would suffer, he says, under his own bad habits. What bad habits? Malcolm's got "an impossible lust" that would only get worse as he devoured all of the maidens of Scotland.

Macduff at first insists there are plenty of maidens in Scotland, and Malcolm would be satisfied.

But Malcolm won't let up talking about how bad a king he'd be, and Macduff finally gives up and admits that Scotland's pretty much doomed.

Once Malcolm sees that Macduff is truly devoted to Scotland rather than just a political alliance, Malcolm goes "psych!": not only is he not lustful, he's never even "known" a woman. And he's got plenty of good qualities. Boo-yah.

So, Macduff, Malcolm and ten thousand Englishmen at their backs get ready to take Scotland back.

Then a doctor shows up (rather unexpectedly) and talks about how King Edward is tending to a crew of poor souls

afflicted by a nasty disease called "scrofula," which the King heals with his touch.

This is why it's helpful to have a genuine king: he gets his power from God and can do cool stuff like cure diseases and rule with an iron fist.

We interrupt this program for a History Snack: Scrofula (what we now know is a form of tuberculosis that affects the lymph nodes and skin) was also called the "King's Evil" and it was thought to be cured by a little something called the "Royal Touch," a kind of laying on of hands ceremony that was performed by monarchs in France and England as far back as the middle ages.

The healing ceremony was supposedly started in England by King Edward the Confessor, Macbeth's ideal king. In a book called The Royal Touch, historian Marc Bloch writes that King James I (who sat on the throne when Macbeth was first written and performed) wasn't exactly thrilled about performing this ceremony —he thought it was superstitious —but he did it anyway.

Ross shows up and chats with Malcolm and Macduff about how Scotland is in a bad way.

Macduff asks after his family, and Ross says they were fine when he left them.

Macduff tells Ross not to be stingy with his words. It feels like he's holding back. So Ross tells him that the rumor is that if Macduff were to return to Scotland, a whole lot of men—and women—would be willing to take up arms against Macbeth.

Malcolm promises when they finally arrive in Scotland, ten thousand English soldiers will come, too.

Ross then announces he has some bad news, actually. Macduff offers to guess at it, but before he does Ross blurts out that, oops, actually Macduff's family has been gruesomely murdered.

It takes a bit for this news to sink in. Macduff asks multiple times if Ross is sure that his wife and kids are all dead.

Macduff blames himself for leaving, but Malcolm recommends that Macduff take his own advice and get his feelings out by murdering rather than weeping.

Macduff vows to slay Macbeth without further delay. He prays for heaven to put him face to face with Macbeth, STAT. Malcolm agrees with this suitably "manly" approach and tells everyone to cheer up: their day will come.

Enter MALCOLM and MACDUFF

MALCOLM
Let us seek out some desolate shade, and there
Weep our sad bosoms empty.
MACDUFF
Let us rather
Hold fast the mortal sword, and like good men
Bestride our down-fall'n birthdom: each new morn
New widows howl, new orphans cry, new sorrows
Strike heaven on the face, that it resounds
As if it felt with Scotland and yell'd out
Like syllable of dolour.
MALCOLM
What I believe I'll wail,
What know believe, and what I can redress,
As I shall find the time to friend, I will.
What you have spoke, it may be so perchance.

This tyrant, whose sole name blisters our tongues,
Was once thought honest: you have loved him well.
He hath not touch'd you yet. I am young; but something
You may deserve of him through me, and wisdom
To offer up a weak poor innocent lamb
To appease an angry god.
MACDUFF
I am not treacherous.
MALCOLM
But Macbeth is.
A good and virtuous nature may recoil
In an imperial charge. But I shall crave your pardon;
That which you are my thoughts cannot transpose:
Angels are bright still, though the brightest fell;
Though all things foul would wear the brows of grace,
Yet grace must still look so.
MACDUFF
I have lost my hopes.
MALCOLM
Perchance even there where I did find my doubts.
Why in that rawness left you wife and child,
Those precious motives, those strong knots of love,
Without leave-taking? I pray you,
Let not my jealousies be your dishonours,
But mine own safeties. You may be rightly just,
Whatever I shall think.
MACDUFF
Bleed, bleed, poor country!
Great tyranny! lay thou thy basis sure,
For goodness dare not cheque thee: wear thou
thy wrongs;
The title is affeer'd! Fare thee well, lord:
I would not be the villain that thou think'st
For the whole space that's in the tyrant's

grasp,
And the rich East to boot.

MALCOLM
Be not offended:
I speak not as in absolute fear of you.
I think our country sinks beneath the yoke;
It weeps, it bleeds; and each new day a gash
Is added to her wounds: I think withal
There would be hands uplifted in my right;
And here from gracious England have I
offer
Of goodly thousands: but, for all this,
When I shall tread upon the tyrant's head,
Or wear it on my sword, yet my poor
country
Shall have more vices than it had before,
More suffer and more sundry ways than
ever,
By him that shall succeed.

MACDUFF
What should he be?

MALCOLM
It is myself I mean: in whom I know
All the particulars of vice so grafted
That, when they shall be open'd, black
Macbeth
Will seem as pure as snow, and the poor
state
Esteem him as a lamb, being compared
With my confineless harms.

MACDUFF
Not in the legions
Of horrid hell can come a devil more damn'd
In evils to top Macbeth.

MALCOLM
I grant him bloody,
Luxurious, avaricious, false, deceitful,
Sudden, malicious, smacking of every sin
That has a name: but there's no bottom,
none,
In my voluptuousness: your wives, your
daughters,
Your matrons and your maids, could not fill
up
The cistern of my lust, and my desire
All continent impediments would o'erbear

That did oppose my will: better Macbeth
Than such an one to reign.

MACDUFF
Boundless intemperance
In nature is a tyranny; it hath been
The untimely emptying of the happy throne
And fall of many kings. But fear not yet
To take upon you what is yours: you may
Convey your pleasures in a spacious plenty,
And yet seem cold, the time you may so
hoodwink.
We have willing dames enough: there
cannot be
That vulture in you, to devour so many
As will to greatness dedicate themselves,
Finding it so inclined.

MALCOLM
With this there grows
In my most ill-composed affection such
A stanchless avarice that, were I king,
I should cut off the nobles for their lands,
Desire his jewels and this other's house:
And my more-having would be as a sauce
To make me hunger more; that I should
forge
Quarrels unjust against the good and loyal,
Destroying them for wealth.

MACDUFF
This avarice
Sticks deeper, grows with more pernicious
root
Than summer-seeming lust, and it hath been
The sword of our slain kings: yet do not
fear;
Scotland hath foisons to fill up your will.
Of your mere own: all these are portable,
With other graces weigh'd.

MALCOLM
But I have none: the king-becoming graces,
As justice, verity, temperance, stableness,
Bounty, perseverance, mercy, lowliness,
Devotion, patience, courage, fortitude,
I have no relish of them, but abound
In the division of each several crime,
Acting it many ways. Nay, had I power, I
should

Pour the sweet milk of concord into hell,
Uproar the universal peace, confound
All unity on earth.
MACDUFF
O Scotland, Scotland!
MALCOLM
If such a one be fit to govern, speak:
I am as I have spoken.
MACDUFF
Fit to govern!
No, not to live. O nation miserable,
With an untitled tyrant bloody-scepter'd,
When shalt thou see thy wholesome days
again,
Since that the truest issue of thy throne
By his own interdiction stands accursed,
And does blaspheme his breed? Thy royal
father
Was a most sainted king: the queen that bore
thee,
Oftener upon her knees than on her feet,
Died every day she lived. Fare thee well!
These evils thou repeat'st upon thyself
Have banish'd me from Scotland. O my
breast,
Thy hope ends here!
MALCOLM
Macduff, this noble passion,
Child of integrity, hath from my soul
Wiped the black scruples, reconciled my
thoughts
To thy good truth and honour. Devilish
Macbeth
By many of these trains hath sought to win
me
Into his power, and modest wisdom plucks
me
From over-credulous haste: but God above
Deal between thee and me! for even now
I put myself to thy direction, and
Unspeak mine own detraction, here abjure
The taints and blames I laid upon myself,
For strangers to my nature. I am yet
Unknown to woman, never was forsworn,
Scarcely have coveted what was mine own,
At no time broke my faith, would not betray

The devil to his fellow and delight
No less in truth than life: my first false
speaking
Was this upon myself: what I am truly,
Is thine and my poor country's to command:
Whither indeed, before thy here-approach,
Old Siward, with ten thousand warlike men,
Already at a point, was setting forth.
Now we'll together; and the chance of
goodness
Be like our warranted quarrel! Why are you
silent?
MACDUFF
Such welcome and unwelcome things at
once
'Tis hard to reconcile.

Enter a Doctor

MALCOLM
Well; more anon.--Comes the king forth, I
pray you?
Doctor
Ay, sir; there are a crew of wretched souls
That stay his cure: their malady convinces
The great assay of art; but at his touch--
Such sanctity hath heaven given his hand--
They presently amend.
MALCOLM
I thank you, doctor.

Exit Doctor

MACDUFF
What's the disease he means?
MALCOLM
'Tis call'd the evil:
A most miraculous work in this good king;
Which often, since my here-remain in
England,
I have seen him do. How he solicits heaven,
Himself best knows: but strangely-visited
people,
All swoln and ulcerous, pitiful to the eye,
The mere despair of surgery, he cures,
Hanging a golden stamp about their necks,

Put on with holy prayers: and 'tis spoken,
To the succeeding royalty he leaves
The healing benediction. With this strange virtue,
He hath a heavenly gift of prophecy,
And sundry blessings hang about his throne,
That speak him full of grace.

Enter ROSS

MACDUFF
See, who comes here?
MALCOLM
My countryman; but yet I know him not.
MACDUFF
My ever-gentle cousin, welcome hither.
MALCOLM
I know him now. Good God, betimes remove
The means that makes us strangers!
ROSS
Sir, amen.
MACDUFF
Stands Scotland where it did?
ROSS
Alas, poor country!
Almost afraid to know itself. It cannot
Be call'd our mother, but our grave; where nothing,
But who knows nothing, is once seen to smile;
Where sighs and groans and shrieks that rend the air
Are made, not mark'd; where violent sorrow seems
A modern ecstasy; the dead man's knell
Is there scarce ask'd for who; and good men's lives
Expire before the flowers in their caps,
Dying or ere they sicken.
MACDUFF
O, relation
Too nice, and yet too true!
MALCOLM
What's the newest grief?
ROSS
That of an hour's age doth hiss the speaker:
Each minute teems a new one.
MACDUFF
How does my wife?
ROSS
Why, well.
MACDUFF
And all my children?
ROSS
Well too.
MACDUFF
The tyrant has not batter'd at their peace?
ROSS
No; they were well at peace when I did leave 'em.
MACDUFF
But not a niggard of your speech: how goes't?
ROSS
When I came hither to transport the tidings,
Which I have heavily borne, there ran a rumour
Of many worthy fellows that were out;
Which was to my belief witness'd the rather,
For that I saw the tyrant's power a-foot:
Now is the time of help; your eye in Scotland
Would create soldiers, make our women fight,
To doff their dire distresses.
MALCOLM
Be't their comfort
We are coming thither: gracious England hath
Lent us good Siward and ten thousand men;
An older and a better soldier none
That Christendom gives out.
ROSS
Would I could answer
This comfort with the like! But I have words
That would be howl'd out in the desert air,
Where hearing should not latch them.
MACDUFF
What concern they?
The general cause? or is it a fee-grief
Due to some single breast?

ROSS
No mind that's honest
But in it shares some woe; though the main part
Pertains to you alone.

MACDUFF
If it be mine,
Keep it not from me, quickly let me have it.

ROSS
Let not your ears despise my tongue for ever,
Which shall possess them with the heaviest sound
That ever yet they heard.

MACDUFF
Hum! I guess at it.

ROSS
Your castle is surprised; your wife and babes
Savagely slaughter'd: to relate the manner,
Were, on the quarry of these murder'd deer,
To add the death of you.

MALCOLM
Merciful heaven!
What, man! ne'er pull your hat upon your brows;
Give sorrow words: the grief that does not speak
Whispers the o'er-fraught heart and bids it break.

MACDUFF
My children too?

ROSS
Wife, children, servants, all
That could be found.

MACDUFF
And I must be from thence!
My wife kill'd too?

ROSS
I have said.

MALCOLM
Be comforted:
Let's make us medicines of our great revenge,
To cure this deadly grief.

MACDUFF

He has no children. All my pretty ones?
Did you say all? O hell-kite! All?
What, all my pretty chickens and their dam
At one fell swoop?

MALCOLM
Dispute it like a man.

MACDUFF
I shall do so;
But I must also feel it as a man:
I cannot but remember such things were,
That were most precious to me. Did heaven look on,
And would not take their part? Sinful Macduff,
They were all struck for thee! naught that I am,
Not for their own demerits, but for mine,
Fell slaughter on their souls. Heaven rest them now!

MALCOLM
Be this the whetstone of your sword: let grief
Convert to anger; blunt not the heart, enrage it.

MACDUFF
O, I could play the woman with mine eyes
And braggart with my tongue! But, gentle heavens,
Cut short all intermission; front to front
Bring thou this fiend of Scotland and myself;
Within my sword's length set him; if he 'scape,
Heaven forgive him too!

MALCOLM
This tune goes manly.
Come, go we to the king; our power is ready;
Our lack is nothing but our leave; Macbeth
Is ripe for shaking, and the powers above
Put on their instruments. Receive what cheer you may:
The night is long that never finds the day.

Exeunt

ACT V

SCENE I. Dunsinane. Ante-room in the castle.

Summary: Back in Scotland, at Macbeth's castle in Dunsinane, a doctor waits with one of Lady Macbeth's gentlewomen.

They're keeping an eye out for Lady Macbeth's sleepwalking, which the gentlewoman reported began once Macbeth left to prepare the house for battle.

Seems like Lady Macbeth has been saying and doing some freaky things on these nightly strolls.Lady Macbeth shows up walking. Make that sleepwalking.

They proceed to watch Lady Macbeth ramble through a tortured speech, at once trying to clean her hands of an imaginary spot (try a little hydrogen peroxide) and nagging at her invisible husband.

All the hand wringing and her question, "Who would have thought the old man to have so much blood in him?" leave little doubt as to what vexes the lady. (This is also where we get the famous line, "Out, damned spot!" so be sure to check out this staged version.)

The doctor says there's nothing he can do to help her, and BTW there are a lot of nasty little rumors floating around.

It sounds like Lady Macbeth probably needs help from a priest, not a doctor.

Enter a Doctor of Physic and a Waiting-Gentlewoman

Doctor

I have two nights watched with you, but can perceive
no truth in your report. When was it she last walked?

Gentlewoman
Since his majesty went into the field, I have seen
her rise from her bed, throw her night-gown upon
her, unlock her closet, take forth paper, fold it,
write upon't, read it, afterwards seal it, and again
return to bed; yet all this while in a most fast sleep.

Doctor
A great perturbation in nature, to receive at once
the benefit of sleep, and do the effects of watching! In this slumbery agitation, besides her
walking and other actual performances, what, at any
time, have you heard her say?

Gentlewoman
That, sir, which I will not report after her.

Doctor
You may to me: and 'tis most meet you should.

Gentlewoman
Neither to you nor any one; having no witness to
confirm my speech.

Enter LADY MACBETH, with a taper

Lo you, here she comes! This is her very guise;
and, upon my life, fast asleep. Observe her; stand close.

Doctor
How came she by that light?

Gentlewoman
Why, it stood by her: she has light by her continually; 'tis her command.

Doctor

You see, her eyes are open.

Gentlewoman
Ay, but their sense is shut.

Doctor
What is it she does now? Look, how she rubs her hands.

Gentlewoman
It is an accustomed action with her, to seem thus
washing her hands: I have known her continue in
this a quarter of an hour.

LADY MACBETH
Yet here's a spot.

Doctor
Hark! she speaks: I will set down what comes from
her, to satisfy my remembrance the more strongly.

LADY MACBETH
Out, damned spot! out, I say!--One: two: why,
then, 'tis time to do't.--Hell is murky!--Fie, my
lord, fie! a soldier, and afeard? What need we
fear who knows it, when none can call our power to
account?--Yet who would have thought the old man
to have had so much blood in him.

Doctor
Do you mark that?

LADY MACBETH
The thane of Fife had a wife: where is she now?--
What, will these hands ne'er be clean?--No more o'
that, my lord, no more o' that: you mar all with
this starting.

Doctor
Go to, go to; you have known what you should not.

Gentlewoman
She has spoke what she should not, I am sure of
that: heaven knows what she has known.

LADY MACBETH
Here's the smell of the blood still: all the
perfumes of Arabia will not sweeten this little
hand. Oh, oh, oh!

Doctor
What a sigh is there! The heart is sorely charged.

Gentlewoman
I would not have such a heart in my bosom for the
dignity of the whole body.

Doctor
Well, well, well,--

Gentlewoman
Pray God it be, sir.

Doctor
This disease is beyond my practise: yet I have known
those which have walked in their sleep who have died
holily in their beds.

LADY MACBETH
Wash your hands, put on your nightgown; look not so
pale.--I tell you yet again, Banquo's buried; he
cannot come out on's grave.

Doctor
Even so?

LADY MACBETH
To bed, to bed! there's knocking at the gate:
come, come, come, come, give me your hand. What's
done cannot be undone.--To bed, to bed, to bed!

Exit

Doctor
Will she go now to bed?

Gentlewoman
Directly.

Doctor
Foul whisperings are abroad: unnatural deeds
Do breed unnatural troubles: infected minds
To their deaf pillows will discharge their secrets:
More needs she the divine than the physician.
God, God forgive us all! Look after her;
Remove from her the means of all annoyance,
And still keep eyes upon her. So, good night:
My mind she has mated, and amazed my sight.
I think, but dare not speak.
Gentlewoman
Good night, good doctor.

Exeunt

SCENE II. The country near Dunsinane.

Summary: A bunch of Scottish noblemen converge in the country near Dunsinane, where Macbeth keeps his castle.

On their heels, heading for Birnam, is the English army, led by Malcolm, Malcom's Uncle Siward, and Macduff. Oh, and a bunch of young Scottish men have taken up arms with the English army.

This is not looking good for Macbeth.

Some dude name Cathness informs the group that the tyrant King is hell-bent on protecting Dunsinane. It's pretty clear that his actions are in his own interests and not the nation's.

Everyone agrees that Macbeth's a lousy king and needs to go.

Drum and colours. Enter MENTEITH, CAITHNESS, ANGUS, LENNOX, and Soldiers

MENTEITH
The English power is near, led on by Malcolm,
His uncle Siward and the good Macduff:
Revenges burn in them; for their dear causes
Would to the bleeding and the grim alarm
Excite the mortified man.
ANGUS
Near Birnam wood
Shall we well meet them; that way are they coming.
CAITHNESS
Who knows if Donalbain be with his brother?
LENNOX
For certain, sir, he is not: I have a file
Of all the gentry: there is Siward's son,
And many unrough youths that even now
Protest their first of manhood.
MENTEITH
What does the tyrant?
CAITHNESS
Great Dunsinane he strongly fortifies:
Some say he's mad; others that lesser hate him
Do call it valiant fury: but, for certain,
He cannot buckle his distemper'd cause
Within the belt of rule.
ANGUS
Now does he feel
His secret murders sticking on his hands;
Now minutely revolts upbraid his faith-breach;
Those he commands move only in command,
Nothing in love: now does he feel his title
Hang loose about him, like a giant's robe
Upon a dwarfish thief.
MENTEITH
Who then shall blame
His pester'd senses to recoil and start,
When all that is within him does condemn
Itself for being there?

CAITHNESS
Well, march we on,
To give obedience where 'tis truly owed:
Meet we the medicine of the sickly weal,
And with him pour we in our country's purge
Each drop of us.
LENNOX
Or so much as it needs,
To dew the sovereign flower and drown the weeds.
Make we our march towards Birnam.

Exeunt, marching

SCENE III. Dunsinane. A room in the castle.

Summary: Macbeth is pumped for battle. Thanks to the sisters' prophecies, he's pretty confident that he can't be beat.

Just then, a messenger enters with the doubtful and fearful news that there are ten thousand somethings marching to Dunsinane.

Somethings? That doesn't sound good.

Macbeth guesses that the somethings are geese. Seriously, dude?

LOL, good try. Actually, they're men coming to kill you.

Macbeth starts to get a little worried. He's had a good run, but it's looking like he won't be relaxing in a peaceful old age.

Lady Macbeth isn't doing too well, either. The doctor reports she isn't sick so much as she is plagued by ill fantasies. Macbeth suggests that the doctor cure her, sooner rather than later.

The doctor replies that the woman's got to fix herself.

By the way, asks Macbeth—does the doctor have the means to purge the English from the countryside of Scotland?

Nope. No amount of money could convince him to stay near the madhouse of Dunsinane.

Enter MACBETH, Doctor, and Attendants

MACBETH
Bring me no more reports; let them fly all:
Till Birnam wood remove to Dunsinane,
I cannot taint with fear. What's the boy Malcolm?
Was he not born of woman? The spirits that know
All mortal consequences have pronounced me thus:
'Fear not, Macbeth; no man that's born of woman
Shall e'er have power upon thee.' Then fly, false thanes,
And mingle with the English epicures:
The mind I sway by and the heart I bear
Shall never sag with doubt nor shake with fear.

Enter a Servant

The devil damn thee black, thou cream-faced loon!
Where got'st thou that goose look?
Servant
There is ten thousand--
MACBETH
Geese, villain!
Servant
Soldiers, sir.
MACBETH
Go prick thy face, and over-red thy fear,
Thou lily-liver'd boy. What soldiers, patch?

Death of thy soul! those linen cheeks of thine
Are counsellors to fear. What soldiers, whey-face?

Servant
The English force, so please you.

MACBETH
Take thy face hence.

Exit Servant

Seyton!--I am sick at heart,
When I behold--Seyton, I say!--This push
Will cheer me ever, or disseat me now.
I have lived long enough: my way of life
Is fall'n into the sear, the yellow leaf;
And that which should accompany old age,
As honour, love, obedience, troops of friends,
I must not look to have; but, in their stead,
Curses, not loud but deep, mouth-honour, breath,
Which the poor heart would fain deny, and dare not. Seyton!

Enter SEYTON

SEYTON
What is your gracious pleasure?

MACBETH
What news more?

SEYTON
All is confirm'd, my lord, which was reported.

MACBETH
I'll fight till from my bones my flesh be hack'd.
Give me my armour.

SEYTON
'Tis not needed yet.

MACBETH
I'll put it on.
Send out more horses; skirr the country round;
Hang those that talk of fear. Give me mine armour.
How does your patient, doctor?

Doctor
Not so sick, my lord,
As she is troubled with thick coming fancies,
That keep her from her rest.

MACBETH
Cure her of that.
Canst thou not minister to a mind diseased,
Pluck from the memory a rooted sorrow,
Raze out the written troubles of the brain
And with some sweet oblivious antidote
Cleanse the stuff'd bosom of that perilous stuff
Which weighs upon the heart?

Doctor
Therein the patient
Must minister to himself.

MACBETH
Throw physic to the dogs; I'll none of it.
Come, put mine armour on; give me my staff.
Seyton, send out. Doctor, the thanes fly from me.
Come, sir, dispatch. If thou couldst, doctor, cast
The water of my land, find her disease,
And purge it to a sound and pristine health,
I would applaud thee to the very echo,
That should applaud again.--Pull't off, I say.--

What rhubarb, cyme, or what purgative drug,
Would scour these English hence? Hear'st thou of them?

Doctor
Ay, my good lord; your royal preparation
Makes us hear something.

MACBETH
Bring it after me.
I will not be afraid of death and bane,
Till Birnam forest come to Dunsinane.

Doctor
[Aside] Were I from Dunsinane away and

clear,
Profit again should hardly draw me here.

Exeunt

SCENE IV. Country near Birnam wood.

Summary: More people meet, specifically Malcolm, Siward, Macduff, Menteith, Caithness, Angus, Lennox, and Ross. Does anyone have a mnemonic for that? (Here you go: My silly mother makes cakes and lemon rinds.)

They hatch a plan: the soldiers will cut down branches to hide themselves under during the march to Dunsinane. Hm. That sounds a lot like the woods of Birnam are about to be on the move.

Many of Macbeth's men have deserted him, and it's clear that those still siding with Macbeth don't believe in the cause.

Still, Macbeth is so set in his certainty of victory that he is willing to let them march right up to Dunsinane, thinking the castle (and he) is protected from harm by the witches' prophecy.

At this point, it might be wise to review that prophecy.

Drum and colours. Enter MALCOLM, SIWARD and YOUNG SIWARD, MACDUFF, MENTEITH, CAITHNESS, ANGUS, LENNOX, ROSS, and Soldiers, marching

MALCOLM
Cousins, I hope the days are near at hand
That chambers will be safe.
MENTEITH
We doubt it nothing.
SIWARD
What wood is this before us?
MENTEITH
The wood of Birnam.
MALCOLM
Let every soldier hew him down a bough
And bear't before him: thereby shall we shadow
The numbers of our host and make discovery
Err in report of us.
Soldiers
It shall be done.
SIWARD
We learn no other but the confident tyrant
Keeps still in Dunsinane, and will endure
Our setting down before 't.
MALCOLM
'Tis his main hope:
For where there is advantage to be given,
Both more and less have given him the revolt,
And none serve with him but constrained things
Whose hearts are absent too.
MACDUFF
Let our just censures
Attend the true event, and put we on
Industrious soldiership.
SIWARD
The time approaches
That will with due decision make us know
What we shall say we have and what we owe.
Thoughts speculative their unsure hopes relate,
But certain issue strokes must arbitrate:
Towards which advance the war.

Exeunt, marching

SCENE V. Dunsinane. Within the castle.

Summary: Macbeth (still at Dunsinane) insists that banners be hung outside the castle.

Many of his former forces are now fighting against him on the English side, making it difficult for him to meet the army in a glorious blaze.

He's still feeling pretty good, since Dunsinane is so fortified that he imagines the enemy army will die of hunger and sickness before he ever even needs to leave the castle.

In the meantime, a shrieking of women tells Macbeth that his wife is dead—it's suicide.

Macbeth here launches into one of Shakespeare's (and literature's) best known and oft-quoted speeches, beginning "She should have died hereafter," meaning one of two things: she would've died eventually so she might as well have died today or, she should have died later because I'm super busy defending the castle right now.

He also gets to say the super famous line, "Life's but a walking shadow [...] a tale told by an idiot full of sound and fury," which is not only an early, maybe the earliest occurrence of Existentialist thought in literature—it's also the basis of William Faulkner's famous work, The Sound and the Fury.

Macbeth is quickly distracted by the news that a "grove" of trees seem to be moving towards Dunsinane, which is all around bad news, since said "grove" is likely Birnam Wood.

Macbeth finally realizes that the prophecy was as twisted as the prophets, but he's going to face the army anyway. If you have to go down, you might as well go down fighting.

Enter MACBETH, SEYTON, and Soldiers, with drum and colours

MACBETH
Hang out our banners on the outward walls;
The cry is still 'They come:' our castle's strength
Will laugh a siege to scorn: here let them lie
Till famine and the ague eat them up:
Were they not forced with those that should be ours,
We might have met them dareful, beard to beard,
And beat them backward home.

A cry of women within

What is that noise?
SEYTON
It is the cry of women, my good lord.

Exit

MACBETH
I have almost forgot the taste of fears;
The time has been, my senses would have cool'd
To hear a night-shriek; and my fell of hair
Would at a dismal treatise rouse and stir
As life were in't: I have supp'd full with horrors;
Direness, familiar to my slaughterous thoughts
Cannot once start me.

Re-enter SEYTON

Wherefore was that cry?
SEYTON
The queen, my lord, is dead.
MACBETH
She should have died hereafter;
There would have been a time for such a word.
To-morrow, and to-morrow, and to-morrow,
Creeps in this petty pace from day to day
To the last syllable of recorded time,

And all our yesterdays have lighted fools
The way to dusty death. Out, out, brief
candle!
Life's but a walking shadow, a poor player
That struts and frets his hour upon the stage
And then is heard no more: it is a tale
Told by an idiot, full of sound and fury,
Signifying nothing.

Enter a Messenger

Thou comest to use thy tongue; thy story
quickly.
Messenger
Gracious my lord,
I should report that which I say I saw,
But know not how to do it.
MACBETH
Well, say, sir.
Messenger
As I did stand my watch upon the hill,
I look'd toward Birnam, and anon,
methought,
The wood began to move.
MACBETH
Liar and slave!
Messenger
Let me endure your wrath, if't be not so:
Within this three mile may you see it
coming;
I say, a moving grove.
MACBETH
If thou speak'st false,
Upon the next tree shalt thou hang alive,
Till famine cling thee: if thy speech be
sooth,
I care not if thou dost for me as much.
I pull in resolution, and begin
To doubt the equivocation of the fiend
That lies like truth: 'Fear not, till Birnam
wood
Do come to Dunsinane:' and now a wood
Comes toward Dunsinane. Arm, arm, and
out!
If this which he avouches does appear,
There is nor flying hence nor tarrying here.

I gin to be aweary of the sun,
And wish the estate o' the world were now
undone.
Ring the alarum-bell! Blow, wind! come,
wrack!
At least we'll die with harness on our back.

Exeunt

SCENE VI. Dunsinane. Before the castle.

Summary: *Malcolm, Siward and Macduff
land their army (covered with branches from
Birnam Wood) outside Dunsinane.*

*Siward will lead the battle with his son, and
Malcolm and Macduff will take the rear and
manage everything else.*

*The soldiers drop their "leafy screens," the
alarms sound, and the battle for Scotland
begins. Rumble!*

BACK NEXT

*Drum and colours. Enter MALCOLM,
SIWARD, MACDUFF, and their Army, with
boughs*

MALCOLM
Now near enough: your leafy screens throw
down.
And show like those you are. You, worthy
uncle,
Shall, with my cousin, your right-noble son,
Lead our first battle: worthy Macduff and
we
Shall take upon 's what else remains to do,
According to our order.
SIWARD
Fare you well.
Do we but find the tyrant's power to-night,
Let us be beaten, if we cannot fight.
MACDUFF

Make all our trumpets speak; give them all breath,
Those clamorous harbingers of blood and death.

Exeunt

SCENE VII. Another part of the field.

Summary: Macbeth appears on stage and compares himself to a bear in a bear-baiting contest (i.e. he's in a serious jam).

History Snack: Bear-baiting is a blood sport that involves chaining a bear to a stake and setting a pack of dogs on it.

Elizabethans thought this was good clean family fun. Bear-baiting arenas were located in the same neighborhoods as the theaters, just in case anyone wanted to take in a play and then top off their day of fun with a little animal cruelty.

Young Siward enters and...quickly dies. Macbeth talks some evil smack over the dead body, to the effect of "your swords and weapons can't touch me because you're of woman born."

Macduff runs on stage looking for Macbeth and screams for the evil tyrant Macbeth to come out and show his ugly face.

Macduff is hot to kill Macbeth with his own sword because he'll likely be haunted by the ghosts of his wife and kids if he doesn't.

He begs "fortune" to let him find Macbeth so he can stab him in the guts.

Siward and Malcolm note that Macbeth's castle has basically been surrendered without a fight. They're winning battles with little effort, mainly because the people they're fighting aren't really trying. Even

Macbeth's soldiers hate him. So. Many. Enemies.

Alarums. Enter MACBETH

MACBETH
They have tied me to a stake; I cannot fly,
But, bear-like, I must fight the course.
What's he
That was not born of woman? Such a one
Am I to fear, or none.

Enter YOUNG SIWARD

YOUNG SIWARD
What is thy name?
MACBETH
Thou'lt be afraid to hear it.
YOUNG SIWARD
No; though thou call'st thyself a hotter name
Than any is in hell.
MACBETH
My name's Macbeth.
YOUNG SIWARD
The devil himself could not pronounce a title
More hateful to mine ear.
MACBETH
No, nor more fearful.
YOUNG SIWARD
Thou liest, abhorred tyrant; with my sword
I'll prove the lie thou speak'st.

They fight and YOUNG SIWARD is slain

MACBETH
Thou wast born of woman
But swords I smile at, weapons laugh to scorn,
Brandish'd by man that's of a woman born.

Exit

Alarums. Enter MACDUFF

MACDUFF
That way the noise is. Tyrant, show thy
face!
If thou be'st slain and with no stroke of
mine,
My wife and children's ghosts will haunt me
still.
I cannot strike at wretched kerns, whose
arms
Are hired to bear their staves: either thou,
Macbeth,
Or else my sword with an unbatter'd edge
I sheathe again undeeded. There thou
shouldst be;
By this great clatter, one of greatest note
Seems bruited. Let me find him, fortune!
And more I beg not.

Exit. Alarums

Enter MALCOLM and SIWARD

SIWARD
This way, my lord; the castle's gently
render'd:
The tyrant's people on both sides do fight;
The noble thanes do bravely in the war;
The day almost itself professes yours,
And little is to do.
MALCOLM
We have met with foes
That strike beside us.
SIWARD
Enter, sir, the castle.

Exeunt. Alarums

SCENE VIII. Another part of the field.

*Summary: Macbeth enters the stage alone
and says he refuses to "play the Roman fool"
(someone who would choose noble suicide
in the face of defeat, like, ahem, Antony).*

*Macduff enters and calls Macbeth a "hell-
hound" and Macbeth talks a little trash in*

*return: I already killed your family so you
best be steppin' back now unless you want
me to have your blood on my hands, too.
Macduff is having none of it.*

*They fight, and Macbeth continues to be
cocky. He says Macduff hasn't got a chance
since he, Macbeth, can't be killed by anyone
"of woman born."*

*That's funny, says Macduff, because
"Macduff was from his mother's womb /
Untimely ripped." In other words: He was
delivered, prematurely, via Cesarean
section. And apparently that means he
wasn't "born." Don't anyone tell Macduff's
mom. Recovering from a medieval C-section
was probably no fun. (Well, to be honest,
she probably died, like the lady whose son,
Robert II, may have been an inspiration for
Macduff.)*

*Macbeth curses the "juggling fiends" and
their twisted prophesy. Now that he knows
he's not invulnerable, he doesn't want to
fight Macduff anymore—but he also doesn't
want to yield. Since he has to pick one, he
decides to keep fighting...right until Macduff
kills him.*

*Malcolm and Siward (the father of the
young man Macbeth recently killed, so we
guess "Old Siward") run across the stage
looking for Macbeth.*

*Siward takes time out to exposit for the
audience: there's a lot of fighting going on
at the castle, the thanes are fighting
exceptionally well, and Malcolm's pretty
close to victory.*

*Malcolm, Siward, Ross, the thanes, and the
soldiers all assess what's been going down
during the battle at the castle.*

It looks like Siward's son (Young Siward) and Macduff are missing.

Ross delivers the news that Young Siward was slain by Macbeth. That's okay, says Young Siward's dad; his wounds were on his front, which means he stood and fought, and that means he died honorably. You know, "like a man."

Things seriously improve when Macduff shows up waving Macbeth's severed head. Everyone turns to Malcolm and yells "Hail, King of Scotland." Hmm. Isn't that how the witches greeted Macbeth back at the beginning of the play?

Malcolm just can't wait to be king. When he is, all the Scottish thanes will be made earls, as in the English system, making them the first earls in Scottish history. Together with Malcolm they'll call home everyone who had to flee the country because of Macbeth's tyranny and punish all of the people who helped the Macbeths.

In his speech, Malcolm also suggests that Lady MacB took her own life, which we didn't really know till now.) But enough death-talk. It's time to party down at the coronation ceremony at Scone. (Mmm...scones.)

Enter MACBETH

MACBETH
Why should I play the Roman fool, and die
On mine own sword? whiles I see lives, the gashes
Do better upon them.

Enter MACDUFF

MACDUFF
Turn, hell-hound, turn!

MACBETH
Of all men else I have avoided thee:
But get thee back; my soul is too much charged
With blood of thine already.

MACDUFF
I have no words:
My voice is in my sword: thou bloodier villain
Than terms can give thee out!

They fight

MACBETH
Thou losest labour:
As easy mayst thou the intrenchant air
With thy keen sword impress as make me bleed:
Let fall thy blade on vulnerable crests;
I bear a charmed life, which must not yield,
To one of woman born.

MACDUFF
Despair thy charm;
And let the angel whom thou still hast served
Tell thee, Macduff was from his mother's womb
Untimely ripp'd.

MACBETH
Accursed be that tongue that tells me so,
For it hath cow'd my better part of man!
And be these juggling fiends no more believed,
That palter with us in a double sense;
That keep the word of promise to our ear,
And break it to our hope. I'll not fight with thee.

MACDUFF
Then yield thee, coward,
And live to be the show and gaze o' the time:
We'll have thee, as our rarer monsters are,
Painted on a pole, and underwrit,
'Here may you see the tyrant.'

MACBETH

I will not yield,
To kiss the ground before young Malcolm's
feet,
And to be baited with the rabble's curse.
Though Birnam wood be come to
Dunsinane,
And thou opposed, being of no woman born,
Yet I will try the last. Before my body
I throw my warlike shield. Lay on, Macduff,
And damn'd be him that first cries, 'Hold,
enough!'

Exeunt, fighting. Alarums

*Retreat. Flourish. Enter, with drum and
colours, MALCOLM, SIWARD, ROSS, the
other Thanes, and Soldiers*

MALCOLM
I would the friends we miss were safe
arrived.
SIWARD
Some must go off: and yet, by these I see,
So great a day as this is cheaply bought.
MALCOLM
Macduff is missing, and your noble son.
ROSS
Your son, my lord, has paid a soldier's debt:
He only lived but till he was a man;
The which no sooner had his prowess
confirm'd
In the unshrinking station where he fought,
But like a man he died.
SIWARD
Then he is dead?
ROSS
Ay, and brought off the field: your cause of
sorrow
Must not be measured by his worth, for then
It hath no end.
SIWARD
Had he his hurts before?
ROSS
Ay, on the front.
SIWARD

Why then, God's soldier be he!
Had I as many sons as I have hairs,
I would not wish them to a fairer death:
And so, his knell is knoll'd.
MALCOLM
He's worth more sorrow,
And that I'll spend for him.
SIWARD
He's worth no more
They say he parted well, and paid his score:
And so, God be with him! Here comes
newer comfort.

*Re-enter MACDUFF, with MACBETH's
head*

MACDUFF
Hail, king! for so thou art: behold, where
stands
The usurper's cursed head: the time is free:
I see thee compass'd with thy kingdom's
pearl,
That speak my salutation in their minds;
Whose voices I desire aloud with mine:
Hail, King of Scotland!
ALL
Hail, King of Scotland!

Flourish

MALCOLM
We shall not spend a large expense of time
Before we reckon with your several loves,
And make us even with you. My thanes and
kinsmen,
Henceforth be earls, the first that ever
Scotland
In such an honour named. What's more to
do,
Which would be planted newly with the
time,
As calling home our exiled friends abroad
That fled the snares of watchful tyranny;
Producing forth the cruel ministers
Of this dead butcher and his fiend-like
queen,

Who, as 'tis thought, by self and violent
hands
Took off her life; this, and what needful else
That calls upon us, by the grace of Grace,
We will perform in measure, time and place:
So, thanks to all at once and to each one,
Whom we invite to see us crowned at Scone.

Flourish. Exeunt Omnes.

FINIS

Glossary:

accompt - account

Acheron - Hell

adage - proverb

afeer'd - confirmed

ague - disease

alarm - trumpet-call

All . . . house - Even if I were to double my efforts on your behalf, it would be nothing compared with the honour you pay by visiting our house.

Angel . . . served - i.e. the Devil

an't - If

antic round - mad dance

aroynt! - begone!

auger-hole - the tiniest crevice

augment - support

augurs. . . blood - Prophecies have (in the past) revealed even the most well-hidden murders

authoriz'd - written

avouch - justify

bark - boat

became him - suited him

become - suit

before - on his chest

beldams - witches

bellman - man who summoned condemned prisoners

Bellona's bridegroom - bridegroom to the goddess of war (i.e. Macbeth).

benison - blessing

borne in hand . . . cross'd - deceived, double-crossed

both the worlds - earth and heaven

brinded - streaked

bruited - announced

card - a sea-chart

cast the water - examine the urine (here, used metaphorically)

chastise - beat off, chase away

cleave - fit

cleave to my consent - approve of my plan

cloudy messenger . . . clogs me with this answer The surly messenger refuses to report to Macbeth the news of Macduff's desertion for fear of punishment.

compassed . . . pearl - surrounded by the elite of Scotland

constrained things - conscripts

construction - intention

convinces . . . art - defeats all the attempts of (medical) skill

corporal - bodily, physical

corporal agent - physical part of myself

cours'd - chased

cow'd - caused me to cower

coz - cousin

crack of doom - Day of Judgment

detraction - self-accusation

dew - wet (with blood)

direction just -exact instructions

disposition . . . owe - my own human nature, courage

divine - priest

dudgeon - handle

effect and it - the result and the plan

Enemy of Man - the Devil

English epicures - the self-indulgent English

enow - enough

equivocator - liar

estate of things - the physical frame of the universe

eternal jewel - immortal soul

excite . . . man - raise the dead

expectation - invitation

eye - command

faculties - kingly powers

fain - rather

farrow - litter of pigs

favour - complexion

feast . . . ceremony - Banquets which are given freely are made more attractive by the "sauce" of ceremony.

fee'd - paid

fee-grief . . . breast - a personal sorrow

fell - terrible

fell of hair - the hair on my flesh

fenny - living in the marshes

fil'd my mind - defiled my guiltless conscience

fitness - appropriateness

flaws and starts - outbursts

flighty . . . with it - Unless acted upon immediately intentions may be overtaken by time.

foisons - abundance

forc'd - reinforced

foreign levy - foreign invasion

gentle weal - noble commonwealth

germens - seeds

gild - paint them with golden blood

gin - trap

gins his reflection - starts to turn in its seasonal course.

go off - perish

golden round - the crown (kingship)

goose -cowardly

Gorgon - hideous monster than turns beholders to stone

gouts - drops

grafted - embedded

Graymalkin, Paddock - grey cat, toad; both "familiars" or witches' assistants

half a soul - a half-wit

harbinger - forerunner

harp'd - guessed

haunt - regularly visit

Hecate - goddess of witchcraft

hie thee hither - come here quickly

holp - helped

hose - trousers

howlet - young owl

husbandry in heaven - the gods are economical with their starlight

I doubt - I am concerned

impress - force

in compt . . . audit - on your account, to be assessed by you

incarnadine - make red

interdiction - accusation

interim - meanwhile

intrenchant - uncuttable

jealousies - suspicions

juggling fiends - deceiving devils (or Fates)

just . . . event - righteous criticism awaits the outcome

jutty . . . vantage - eaves, convenient corner

kerns, Gallowglasses - light infantry, heavy infantry.

lapp'd in proof - covered in armor.

latch - catch

lave our honours . . . streams - show ourselves to be honourable by washing ourselves in acts of flattery

lees - dregs

lime - bird lime (a sticky substance for trapping birds)

line the rebel . . . vantage - secretly give aid to the rebels.

list - tournament

lodg'd - beaten down

lose the dues - miss the reward

love . . . love - As king, I must always acknowledge my subjects' love even though doing so is a burden to me. But I must tell you that in taking trouble for me, you win God's thanks.

loved mansionry - favorite building

made a shift to cast him - with effort I overpowered the drink

magot-pies - magpies

marry - indeed

mated - amazed

maws - appetites

metaphysical - supernatural

mettle - courage

minions of their race - best of their breed

minutely - every minute

mortal custom - usual lifespan

mounch'd - munched

napkins - handkerchiefs

near in blood . . . bloody - close relations are more likely to be suspected of murder

oblivious - that brings oblivion

old - frequent

ornament of life - the crown

pains - service to me

palter - toy with

parricide - murder of a parent

particular addition - a specific title

pauser - restraining force of

pendent - hanging

penthouse lid - eyelid.

physic - medicine

practice - medical expertise

prate - prattle

probation - approval

procreant cradle - nest

protest me - claim that I am

purpose . . . purveyor - intended to arrive before him

quarry . . . deer - carnage of these dead creatures

rancours - bitterness

ravin - eat up

rebuked - mocked

receipt . . . limbeck - container for an alchemist's solution; here, Macbeth's plan

recoil in an imperial charge - recoil (like a cannon) when under royal orders (from Macbeth)

rendered - surrendered

rhubarb . . . drug - purgatives

rich East to boot - all the wealth of the Orient as well

roofed - surmounted

unyon - hag

avage - bold

cotch'd - injured

cruples - doubts

econd course - that is, at the banquet of life

ecurity - overconfidence

ere - dry

hoal - sandbank

houghs, water-rugs - rough-coated dogs

ightless couriers - invisible winds

inel - Macbeth's father.

kirr - scour

leights - charms

ooth - truthfully

pacious plenty - at will

peculation - eyesight

tamp - coin

ticking-place - its limit

traight - straightaway

uborn'd - bribed

ummer-seeming - youthful

urcease - death

urfeited - drunk

sway - command

swelling act . . . theme - the developing royal drama

taking-off - murder

Tarquin - murderous king of Rome

temple-haunting martlet - bird that nests in church porches

their charge - that is, Duncan

this great King - possibly a reference to James I (the king in Shakespeare's audience)

to friend -auspicious

trains - tricks

trammel up - obstruct, prevent

travelling lamp - the sun

treatise - tale

trifled - made trivial

trifles - trivial gifts

two delinquents - that is, the guards of Duncan's chamber

undivulg'd pretence - undisclosed plot of treason

unshrinking station - unyielding position

upbraid . . . faith-breach - rebuke his broken promises

utterance - utmost

vault - wine cellar, *punning on* grave

verities - true predictions

vizards - masks

want the thought - help thinking

wants - requires

warrant in that theft - this kind of stealing (away) is justified

wassail - entertainment

which is not us'd for you - which you are not used to

with Him above . . . work - with God's help

yesty - frothing

Macbeth cuts Macdonwald in half   Motifs

-Chops head & hangs it up   "foul & fair"

Duncan & Macbeth = Cousins

With it Killing pigs
Do not mess with witches
Fat women eating chestnuts
& Sailing across ocean and will kill the beforehand.

Made in the USA
Middletown, DE
29 January 2021